The Sky Always Hears Me

Sixteen-year-old Morgan lives in a hick town in the middle of Nebraska. College is two years away. Her mom was killed in a car accident when she was three, her dad drinks, and her stepmom is a non-entity. Her boyfriend Derek is boring and her coworker Rob has a very cute butt that she can't stop staring at. Then there's the kiss she shared with her neighbor Tessa.

But when Morgan discovers that the one person in the world she trusted most has kept a devastating secret from her, Morgan must redefine her life and herself.

This book is for Dan and Shae,
Doris Evelyn Nylander Cronn Patterson Nielsen-Eltoft,
and the TaTas, my sisters in ink,
for teaching me how and telling me I could.

Kirstin Cronn - Mills

the
sky
always
hears
me

and the hills don't mind

flux
™
Woodbury, Minnesota

First Edition
First Printing, 2009

Book design by Steffani Sawyer
Cover design by Ellen Dahl
Cover image © Stockbyte (model) and Digital Stock (sky)

Flux, an imprint of Llewellyn Publications

Library of Congress Cataloging-in-Publication Data
Cronn-Mills, Kirstin, 1968–
  The sky always hears me : and the hills don't mind / Kirstin Cronn-Mills.—1st ed.
      p. cm.
  Summary: Sixteen-year-old Morgan struggles with her growing attraction to a co-worker, her unsatisfactory relationship with her boyfriend, and with her own sexual orientation after a girlfriend is rumored to be gay.
  ISBN 978-0-7387-1504-9
  [1. Dating (Social customs)—Fiction. 2. Lesbians—Fiction.] I. Title.
  PZ7.C88149Sk 2009
  [Fic]—dc22

                                        2009016292

Flux
Llewellyn Publications
A Division of Llewellyn Worldwide, Ltd.
2143 Wooddale Drive, Dept. 978-0-7387-1504-9
Woodbury, MN 55125-2989, U.S.A.
www.fluxnow.com

Printed in the United States of America

Acknowledgments

Many people deserve my thanks: Steve Deger, for introducing me to the real Morgan; the real Tessa, for starting this story; the real Grocery Yurt, plus Kjell, Scott, and the Mo Fo Stocker's Cart; Stephen Lin, whoever he is, for his funky Chinese restaurant name generator; the TaTas, for hours and hours of time spent with Morgan; Dan & Shae, for patience, kindness, and the ability to keep me grounded; Tammy Mason as well as Elza McGaffin, for important character help; George Nicholson, for assistance with earlier drafts of this book; Andrew Karre, for saying "what else do you have?" and then teaching me how to shape a novel; Hannah Frantz, for being the best beta reader a girl could wish for; and everyone at Flux who made this book into something wonderful, including Brian Farrey, Sandy Sullivan, Courtney Kish, Steven Pomije, Ellen Dahl, and Steffani Sawyer. I am grateful to all of you.

The hills save me, but I would never say that out loud. I hate this place. So I should hate the hills, right? But I don't.

Today it's *ALIENS, TAKE ME NOW*, fifteen times, shouted into the air. Then *I AM INSANE* and *DIE ASS-HOLE DIE* and *BITE ME*, but only five times each.

Consolidate your interests
while the lights are active.

Tom Yun Fun's, Minneapolis

Right now, I'm supposed to be stocking candy. There are bags and bags of M&Ms, plain and peanut, sitting on my conveyor belt. The store is empty, which is nice, so I take my time. The bags become piles, and then the plain M&Ms become a house, with a doghouse made of peanut ones behind it. I try not to stare at Rob as he stocks cigarettes. I know I'm supposed to be faithful to Derek, and I am. Just not in my mind.

"Morgan!"

"What?" My plain-M&M house falls over.

Rob grins. "Come help me stock cigarettes." I wander over while he studies me. "You must be thinking very serious thoughts."

I am not going to tell him the truth: I was pondering his very cute ass, which he displayed as he was working on the smokes. Where has that ass been all my life?

"Just contemplating fortunes."

"Pardon me?" He hands me a carton of cigarettes.

"You know—inside fortune cookies?" I open the carton and shake out the packs. The Salem Ultra Lights slide into their spot.

"That's a weird thing to think about." He hands me another carton.

"Not as strange as pondering something like, I don't know, foam fingers. People do that, too, and that's way weirder."

"Like the 'We're Number One' foam fingers? How are those weird?" He seems to have taken personal offense.

"Fortunes are way more useful."

"How could a fortune be useful? Besides that, where can you get fortunes around here?"

"In the deli." I point toward the back of the store. There's no Chinese restaurant in Central Nowhere, of course. "But what if a fortune told you how to make a million bucks? You never know."

"That's the dumbest thing I've ever heard."

"You just have no imagination." Even though I've only known him for a few weeks, I smack him on the arm. Usually I save smacking for close friends.

He rubs the spot where I connected. "I bet you don't have any friends. You hit."

He intoxicates me. He invigorates me. He makes me think of obnoxious, hokey verbs like *invigorates*.

Since I was so busy looking at his lovely face, I put the Winstons in with the Marlboro Reds. But now Rob and the Winstons have to wait, because Crazy Gus is unloading groceries on my conveyor belt. Wow, does he need a shower. He smells like pee and dirt and feet, all at the same time. Cigars, Chex, and cat food. Must be a *C* evening at Crazy Gus's house.

After Gus is gone, I go back to the candy because Rob's done with the smokes. He fixed the Winstons after a glare in my direction. While I roll the Rolos into the right place, I see Rob sneaking glances at me from over by the corn, where he's stocking the special of the week—creamed, for forty-nine cents a can.

For value, buy the creamed corn.

I can imagine the look on someone's face when that falls out of a cookie.

It really is strange to want to write fortunes for a living. But people attach meaning to strange things and listen to all sorts of advice they shouldn't, so why not convince them to buy creamed corn? It's my dream to write the Great American Novel, but I've got to do something while I perfect my masterpiece. Fortunes are as good as anything else. No one will ever know it's me writing them, but that's probably okay.

For good luck, do not go to work on Tuesdays.

To find love, look under the couch.

I wonder if more people would stay home on Tuesdays or look under their couch.

I hope fortune writers make more money than poets.

It's a million degrees in Central Nowhere, because it's August 1st and global warming is turning everything into a desert. I work in a grocery store. My boyfriend is boring. My dad and stepmom, Brad and Anne Callahan, suck in an unbelievable way. College is two years away. I live in a hick town. We'll run out of fossil fuels in twenty years, but no one will let me use the car before it happens. Rob is right: I don't really have friends, just Girls I Sit By At Lunch. My mom died when I was almost three. My grandma is the coolest woman in this town. And I have to get a new life before I go crazy.

Stick it up your ass.

The fortune cookie factory had better supervise me, or they'll get hate mail.

I watch Rob for a while longer. He's a bit of a novelty, because he's only been here a few months. He's the new assistant-something-or-other manager, but I've yet to see him manage anything. He's moved on to baked beans, down at the far end of the aisle, and he's bent over again, showing me that excellent butt.

I bet he collects foam fingers.

*Your attention to detail is both
a blessing and a curse.*

Hot Pot Restaurant, Hong Kong

Mrs. Anderson stalks away, glaring at me after our little exchange about the price of a gallon of milk. Yes, it's more expensive than it was in 1968, when the store opened. Yes, the price is correct. No, I don't put the extra money in my pocket. I smile as she throws me one more daggered look over her shoulder, because I maintain an air of professionalism at all times. But I imagine myself ramming a full grocery cart into her car. If I did it right—with the correct angle, enough space, and repeated rammings—I could scratch my initials in her door.

Just shut up and work.

I am silently, calmly, casually stocking peaches. I am also listening for any good dirt. Gossip is one of the perks of this job. Since people don't even notice you're there, you hear crazy things. One time I heard two teachers from the high school talking about Mr. Hamilton and Mrs. Rogers doing it in the teacher's lounge. I didn't stay hidden that day because I was laughing so loud. But so were they.

6

*Her breasts heaved. A whiteboard marker
quivered between her toes as he slowly locked the
door.*

*"Are you ready to be my student?" his voice
growled, over the unwashed coffee cups and the
papers scattered across the floor.*

*She sighed. "Of course, you big strong teacher.
Take me now!"*

*The old saggy couch groaned under the weight
of their passion.*

I can put it in my novel.

I am moving cans of fruit around when interesting
sounds drift over the top of the shelves.

"I cannot believe that … Tessa and Amanda?"

"She looks so lesbian, with that weird hair. We should've
known."

I almost drop my peaches.

"Amanda? That can't be right."

"Believe it. Amanda's mom found them."

"Oh my gosh!"

I peek around the corner, and two moms are parked
in front of the salad dressing and relishes, gabbing away.
I sneak over to find out more, but the case of pickles I
grabbed for camouflage falls out of my fingers and crashes
all over everything. Then the whole aisle smells like vin-
egar, and while I'm sweeping up the glass and mopping
the floor, I cut my finger open, so blood mixes with the
pickle juice. It's just gross.

The moms are long gone by the time I get things

cleaned up, which is probably good. I'd be very obvious, following them around the store.

Tessa's in my class. She's also my neighbor, and I know exactly what those women are talking about.

Two Friday nights ago, sometime around one a.m., I was spacing out in my back yard, lying on a blanket and contemplating the stars. Then I heard Tessa's back door open—her house is across the alley from mine—and I saw her start heading my way. It was easy to tell she was drunk, because she walked no straight lines in her path toward me. I don't know how she knew I was there, but she plopped herself on my blanket and began to tell me about her evening. I listened, but I kept watching the stars.

And then she leaned over and kissed me.

Up to that point, I had no idea she liked girls. In Central Nowhere, people don't go there. Boys like girls and girls like them back, and that's all you need to know.

The problem was I kissed her back.

It felt good. Really, really, really good. We locked lips and tongues and swapped all these vibes, and it felt excellent and horribly wrong all at the same time.

Then she stumbled to her feet, without a word, and lurched back to her house.

I lay on the blanket for a long time after that.

A man who lives only for pleasure is a poor man.

The Ultimate Noodle, Cincinnati

I am working and trying to blank my mind, trying not to think about Tessa or the back yard, trying not to be pissed that Ingrid and Jessica, the Girls I Sit By At Lunch Most Often, drove to Kearney without me when they know that I'll do anything to get out of this town, even driving fifty miles to the nearest Target. Then Derek comes in and buys French onion dip and chips, a two-liter of Mountain Dew, and some hot dogs. No buns. Of course he comes through my checkout line.

Derek has beautiful eyes, wavy hair, and big muscles. He's cute but dumb, like a bunny. We sat next to each other in study hall when I was in ninth grade and he was in tenth, and one day he realized I could help him with his math homework. Then he noticed I had nice boobs, so he asked me out. The rest is history.

I know everyone thinks we're a strange couple—the nerdy brain and the dumb jock—but I keep him around to help with my social handicap, because it's at least nine zillion. With him my social handicap goes down to two or so, because the gorgeous-jock status is a double bonus, though I'm not sure why I care. He keeps me around because he doesn't know what else to do. But I also think he genuinely likes me. And I genuinely like him. Mostly.

He smiles his killer smile. "How are you, good-lookin'?"

I push each piece of junk food over the sensor, beep beep beep. "Thought you were going out tonight with your buds."

"We're staying home to watch wrestling. Come over when you're done."

Think what his breath will be like then.

I try to look cute so he won't be pissed. "I have to work early tomorrow."

"That sucks. See you tomorrow night?"

"You got it." I smile, and hope it's convincing.

He stops to think. "Hold it. I start football practice tomorrow night. After that?"

"Pick me up when you're done." I give him another semi-convincing smile.

He leans over and gives me a quick kiss, then waltzes out the door with a wave. Already his breath is not so good, so I'm glad I get to skip the after-chips-and-dip-and-hotdogs version.

Those muscles got me hooked, and then I noticed the smile and realized he's funny, so that sealed the deal. But he's in the bottom third of his class, and he's not one for reading, which to me is like saying you're not one for breathing. He intends to work for his father's construction company after high school and set himself up with a nice house, a nice truck, and a nice life, with no desire to see anything outside of the boundaries of Central Nowhere. And I want to see to the edge of the world.

I watch Derek through the window. He's walked across the parking lot and is laughing with the people at Kwik Gas, also known as Gas & Ass. Once you get into high school, you discover that Gas & Ass is the place to be—all plans and announcements get made there, from who's having the fiesta to who's hooking up with whom (it's the ultimate proof of my nerdhood—I used the word *whom*). A shared parking lot isn't a bad thing: you stop at Gas & Ass, find out where the party is, then wander over here to buy Coke for your vodka and chips for your pot munchies. Kwik Gas and Food Pride. Gas & Ass and Any Other Name But Food Pride.

Derek's being his social-butterfly self, and the women are eating it up. I'm not sure whether I care.

> *Derek swept Morgan into his arms. And then he stood there, because he didn't know what to do. So he dropped her.*
>
> *Morgan picked herself up off the floor. "Yeah, well, your breath stinks and you're stupid. Get out of my sight."*

Maybe I should write cautionary fortunes.

Do not fall in love with great hair and big muscles.

Like anyone would listen.

And then there's our sex life: boring. Or, to use my dictionary-ness, *uninteresting, tedious, dull, mind-numbing, lackluster, dreary, tiresome, monotonous, unexciting, wearisome, repetitive, humdrum,* and *uninspiring.*

He's got a big black 1994 Buick, and the front seat is as big as a sofa, though much more slippery. We park it on the same dead-end street every Friday and Saturday night and turn the radio to one of the three kinds of stations we get out here: easy listening, country, or talk. Yuck. Usually we pick easy listening, because on that station no one accidentally gives out a "yee haw!" at an inopportune moment.

We kiss for a while, though never long enough, and that part's fantastic, because (1) Derek is an inspired participant in that activity, and (2) I believe in kissing. It's one of the best things ever invented, any kind, all kinds. Eskimo kisses, your basic smooch, deep tongue wrestling, air kisses—whatever way you can do it. It can be impartial, or it can be the most intimate gesture around.

Which is why I have no idea what it means that I kissed Tessa back. Too many options for interpretation.

Nobody in my bio fam kisses each other except for me and Grandma.

While we're locking lips, Derek runs his hand up and down the front of my shirt, and he's very gentle but insistent, so he gets my heart—and the rest of me—humming quite nicely. I'm always ready for something gentle and slow, but everything goes downhill from there. Clothes fly everywhere, and I fake it—lots of moans and groans and "oh yes!"—but usually I feel nothing. I always figure I should make union scale for my acting job.

Watch out for bad sex. If you're sure it's bad, that is.

Maybe it's really okay sex, and I'm just not paying attention. But I know I should feel more than bored. And Derek's anatomy is *nothing* like the guys in *Playgirl*, either. Jessica and Ingrid bought one when they went to Kearney, and those are some gigantic penises if the photos are real. I know Derek can't help what he was given, but I wonder. Maybe you need to use your little penis in a big way. Maybe I need to read to him, or to his penis.

I also wonder about sex in a bed. It has to be better than sex in a front seat.

Do not have sex in a car.

Do not have sex after boring dates.

In my mind, I am always in a room with roses, with someone who makes shivers run up and down my body like the guys women swoon over in all the cheesy date movies that Ingrid and Jessica make me watch. There is mucho kissing and we are doing what I want to do, even though I'm not sure what that is right now, with my limited repertoire.

Sometimes I'm with Jack Sparrow, ooh la la. Sometimes I'm with Rob. No matter who it is, Derek is nowhere to be found. Nor, for the record, is Tessa.

Derek's still standing at the Gas & Ass, and there's a circle of women around him, then a circle of men around the women. The men look very crabby. The women look very happy.

I should look elsewhere.

> Soon you will be sitting on top of the world.
>
> Ron's Won Ton, San Francisco

It's not quite the top of the world, but it's high enough for me.

My town is in the middle of a thirty-mile-wide river valley that was created a million bazillion years ago. The only thing left of that giant river is two forks of the Platte River that are each less than a hundred yards wide. I cannot even fathom (no pun intended) a river that's thirty miles wide. Imagine the size of the fish.

When I'm feeling freaky, I borrow my grandma's car and drive out to the hills that form the edge of the valley. I park at the top of a hill and walk a ways. Then I yell, things like *I AM A SECRET SEX FIEND*, which seems obvious, and *I HATE EVERYBODY*, which I mostly do, and *I'M A LOSER*, which is true, because I can't manage to have friends except Girls I Sit By At Lunch, and *I HATE MY JOB*, which isn't quite right, because Rob is there. Sometimes I do a war dance and howl. Sometimes I roll around on the ground, but it takes a long time to pick off the dead grass when I'm done, so I don't do it a lot.

Sometimes I sit and look. I look at my town. I look at the town ten miles west of my town. I look at the sky. I imagine what it will be like to leave here, and my heart sings a little.

When I take Grandma's car back, she always says, "Do you feel better now?" She knows what I do out there. And I say, "Yes." And she says, "You can borrow my car any time you want," because my grandma is the coolest woman on the planet, and the only person on this planet I trust, for that matter. And she knows I need the space that is the thirty-mile-wide river valley, and she wants me to be happy.

Be positive.

Wong Foo's, New York City

As August progresses in central Nebraska, all the grass dies and it stays so yellow and hot that if you go outside, your brain turns into a puddle and runs out your eyeballs. Too gross for me. So I'm reading inside at the kitchen table instead of in the yard. Really I'm watching Tessa's house and pretending to read, also pretending not to care what I heard at the grocery store. I haven't heard it again from any other gossipy moms, nor have I heard anything at the Gas & Ass. Nobody would believe it anyway. That kind of stuff doesn't happen around here. Right?

Then the phone rings. Since my parents do not believe in caller ID, I tend to answer it.

"Uh … Morgan."

The voice is familiar, but I can't place it.

"Morgan?"

"Yeah?"

"It's Tessa."

Silence on my end.

She plunges on. "I need your help." She's not her usual loud self.

"Excuse me?" I have no earthly idea how I could help her.

"My parents want me to take the ACT, and they want me to study with someone."

"Why me?"

"You're the smartest girl I know, and you live behind me."

Here's the thing: we're barely friends, even though we're both juniors, because Tessa is a jock as well as a party girl, and I like books. As you might imagine, the gulf between us is rather large.

I draw circles on the pad of paper next to the phone. "When do you need to start?"

"Next week?"

I write *next week* and *Tessa* on the pad. "Okay."

"Okay." She hangs up. No "thank you," no nothing.

On the social ladder of high school, Tessa's at the top. She plays volleyball, basketball, and softball, and letters in everything, and I couldn't letter in tying people's shoes. She also knows all the buyers, has the best dope, and has a zillion friends. If you wanted to take a drunken joyride or bungee jump off the nearest high bridge, she's your girl. She's probably not really interested in going to college—I'd bet her mom is making her take the ACT—but even if she flunks out she'll be the center of attention wherever she goes, so it won't matter.

My social standing is a million rungs lower than Tessa's

because nobody in this town cares about brains, and acknowledging you're smart is like claiming you had elf ears grafted onto your regular ears. A few people think it's great, but most people think it's uber-weird.

You will be accosted by a neighbor wearing elf ears.

I write it down on the pad of paper and tuck the whole thing into the napkins on the table. Let someone else ponder it.

None of the secrets of success will work
unless you do.

China Pot Stickers, Cleveland

A week later, when Tessa comes over, I study her hair while she flops into the chair. It's spiky all over her head, maybe longer in back than in the front, with bleached white tips at the moment. Sometimes they're purple. It's kind of jock hair, kind of cool hair. Lesbian hair? Could be. How do those moms know what lesbian hair is? Have they ever seen Portia de Rossi? She's got better hair than they do, and she's a lesbian. In fact, Ellen DeGeneres has better hair than those moms.

I make sure to sit across the table from Tessa, and I absolutely do not look her in the face. "So ... we need to study."

Tessa clears her throat. "Yeah ... want to hear the joke I told my softball girls?" She coaches a middle school team.

"Sure."

"Why did Cinderella get kicked off the team?" She's examining our salt and pepper shakers.

"I don't know. Why?" I'm studying the place mats.

Her smile is forced when she looks at me. "Because she ran from the ball!"

I make my voice sound much calmer than I feel. "So...when?"

"When what?" She's alarmed. She's forgotten why she's here?

"When do you want to study with me?" It obviously isn't today.

The deer-in-the-headlights look disappears. "Oh...I have no idea. Can we do it every week or so?"

I kick the table leg with the toe of my flip-flop. "Do you have some of those study guides?"

"My mom will get 'em."

Kick kick kick. "There's not much time. School starts really soon."

Tessa sighs. "I hate school."

"So why are you thinking about college?"

"How else do I get out of this town?" She stands up. "Thanks. Gotta go." And she practically runs out my back door.

After she leaves, I call Jessica. She is a good Girl To Sit By because she knows everything about everyone.

"Have you heard any rumors about Tessa lately?"

She squeals. "Oooh, yeah!"

"What?"

Clearly she's imparting state secrets, because her whisper is almost too soft to hear. "Well, my mom told me that Amanda's mom found Amanda and Tessa in bed. Together. Naked."

"Holy shit."

"You think my mom is a liar?" Her voice raises twenty decibels.

"No, I'm … wondering how that could happen." Which is a lie.

"How should I know? It must've been a slumber party."

I don't choose that moment to enlighten her. "I can't imagine anything else, I guess."

"Well, you know Tessa. It's not like she's … like us." Jessica's disdain for anyone not like her is legendary.

"So how are we?"

"We're normal!"

"Gotta go, Jessica." The best part of a conversation with Jessica is hanging up.

Tomorrow is junior-year orientation, which means I have two weeks of freedom left. I'll sit with Jessica and Ingrid, even though it's not lunch. And she's right: Tessa's not like us. She's bigger than us, more popular than us, a superstar in this one-horse town. We are only serfs. Which isn't bad, as long as we don't have to do any manual labor. And Tessa's a lesbian, which makes her a palm tree in the middle of Central Nowhere—exotic and strange. And suspicious.

> Life is both complicated
> and simple at the same time.
>
> Huhot's, Phoenix

I'm messing around in the baking aisle making a display of frosting, and two freshmen girls come wandering by, giggling like the dingbats they are. When they see me, their eyes get as big as jelly doughnuts and they slide down the side of the aisle opposite me, flattening their bodies against the shelves as they go by. I stare, because I don't know what else to do, but when they leave the aisle, I stalk them.

I finally figure out what they're talking about by hiding behind a rack of hot dog buns, right next to the deli. They're picking out fried chicken and discussing the Amanda/Tessa rumor, which makes sense because Amanda's a freshman, too.

Blue Bikini Top Girl is ordering. "So they were naked? Eeew! Uh, yeah, we'd like six pieces of white meat."

Yellow Dress is just along for the ride. "Amanda's mom thought something was up." She studies the rest of the chicken pieces as Sue, the deli lady, sticks some in a box with lightning speed. Sue has no time for freshmen girls.

Yellow Dress doesn't notice. "They were spending way too much time together."

"But Amanda said they were just friends." Blue Bikini takes the chicken from Sue.

Yellow Dress checks out the doughnuts. "Don't ask me. I thought Tessa's girlfriend was the girl back there, with the frosting."

Blue Bikini frowns. "I heard that, too. But then I heard Tessa and Amanda have been dating for six months, so when would Tessa have time for Frosting Girl?"

Yellow Dress opens the chicken box in Blue Bikini's hands. "I dunno. Is this enough chicken?"

"I think so. Let's go—they're waiting for us."

And they head off to check out with their chicken and the potato chips they've grabbed from Aisle 12.

I stand by the hot dog rack for a long time.

It was one a.m. How could anybody know?

"Is there a reason you're hiding behind the bread?" This comment is followed by a chuckle.

I whirl around to see Rob, whose arms are full of bread racks. For some reason he doesn't have on the requisite white button-down shirt today, just a T-shirt. And the man has pipes, it's obvious. Plus there's part of a tattoo hanging out of one sleeve.

"None of your biz, and why are you delivering bread? Don't we have a bread guy?"

"Sometimes I fill in for him on his route. I have a thousand jobs, it feels like." He sets the bread racks on the floor and proceeds to sort through what's on the shelves.

"Where else do you work?"

"With my dad on the farm, then here at the store, and with the bread people. And I serve drinks at the Elks on the weekends."

"You're not twenty-one!"

"You only have to be nineteen to serve—twenty-one to bartend." He throws me a loaf. "Care to be useful?"

I help him get the wheat, white, and whole-grain in their space without squishing too much of it. His tattoo keeps winking at me, there and not there at the edge of his sleeve.

"What's your ink?"

"Which one?" He shuffles the bread into its spaces.

"Your arm."

He stops and pulls up the cloth. "This one's a dragon." It's very stylized, full of lines and very intense. Then he turns around and pulls his T-shirt away from his shoulder, showing me a big-winged bird almost lifting off his skin. "This one's a phoenix." It's also lines, tribal like the dragon. He rearranges his shirt. "I have three others, two you can't see in a grocery store aisle." His grin invites me to ask where they are.

I decide to play it safe. "Do they mean anything?" I gawk at the tail of the dragon hanging out of his sleeve. I had no idea tattoos could be so sexy.

"The dragon is for strength—it's my Chinese zodiac symbol—and the phoenix is to remind me that I'll always be reborn."

"You need to be reborn?" This is a new twist.

"More like rise to the top. Get what I want. That kind of stuff." He's counting loaves of bread and stacking empty trays. "I got the dragon before I went to Argentina, and I got the phoenix while I was there, to remind me of my trip. And look at this." He bends down and hikes up his pant leg. Right above his ankle there's a cow skull, like the ones you see in Old West advertisements in Western Nowhere.

"Not to go backwards, but Argentina?"

He starts throwing bread again. "I went there for my senior year."

"Oh yeah. Right." I knew that, actually, because I'd asked around when he showed up as our assistant faux manager.

Imagine being able to go away.

I study his ankle. "How is a cow skull any less weird than fortunes? And why a cow?"

He drops his pants leg. "I see cows every day, and they're way cooler than fortunes, and I went to Argentina to visit cows because they talk less than people do." He gives me one more grin, picks up his bread trays, and disappears around the corner.

I go back to my baking aisle. Boss Man Steve comes by.

"What's new today, Morgan?"

"Not much. Just frosting the cake aisle."

He laughs. "Good one." He touches my arm with a look that says, "too bad you're sixteen, or I'd ask you out."

I give him back a look that says "I'm a nerd, not a desperate fool," and he goes away.

Traffic's starting to pick up. Mr. Miller, the chorus teacher, goes by, humming something I'm sure people will be learning in a few weeks. Ed the Mail Guy almost hits me with his cart. He's just as reckless with his mail truck. And Crazy Gus totters into the aisle but totters back out before he makes it down to me. I peer into his cart before he turns around and see peanuts, plums, and Purple Zoom cleaner. Maybe he thinks there are no *P* foods in the baking aisle. What about pumpkin?

My mind won't quit wondering where Rob's other tattoos are.

Beautiful words are not always truthful.
Truthful words are not always beautiful.

Speedy Asian Paradise, Chicago

I love the word *bitchrod*. It's so surfer '80s. "Morgan, how are you?" "I'm bitchrod, thank you!" And *deranged*. I like the lurching quality of that word. It sounds like a serial killer with a crazy eye who drags his foot through the mud. "The deranged high school junior stood up to give her speech."

Beware of deranged and/or bitchrod lesbians hidden in your town.

I write it on a piece of notebook paper, in really big letters, then fold it into a paper airplane and sail it high up into a tree.

Of course, the football scrimmage is less than interesting. But it's something to do, I can walk here, and Derek is playing, so I should be the dutiful girlfriend and watch. I'm standing talking to Ingrid and Jessica and Tessa walks up. Ingrid and Jessica stop talking to give her a look.

I will myself not to run away. "Hey, Tessa."

"You got my mom off my back." She's standing there like the social force she is, surrounded by the volleyball team, who are chatting amongst themselves while waiting for their leader to lead again.

"How?"

"She thinks we study every week."

"Oh. Well." So what is she doing when she's supposed to be studying with me?

"So ... thanks." Tessa smiles, punches me on the shoulder—her traditional affection gesture—and walks off with the team. She's the center of attention again.

Ingrid ponders me. "You two are friends all of a sudden?"

"Uh ... sort of."

Jessica shoots an ugly look toward Tessa's back. "I bet those rumors are true."

"Which ones?" I feel my insides threaten to spill out.

"The ones about her and Amanda." Jessica slurps her soda with gusto. "Creepy."

"How is that creepy?" I can't believe I'm defending her.

"Because ... " Jessica huffs. "Because she's got weird hair."

I laugh. "What does her hair have to do with anything? That's what the moms said, too."

Ingrid looks interested. "What moms?"

"The ones I overheard in Grocery Galaxy, talking about Tessa."

Jessica smirks at me. "See? It's not just my mom. Tessa's weird."

"So what?" My stomach decides to stay where it is, so I walk toward the stands. "What's it to you?"

Ingrid follows along. "No biggie to me."

I'm so glad she said that.

While the three of us sit and watch the game, I keep my eye on Tessa. She's laughing and joking with the volley-ball girls, and I am grateful to heaven no one can see inside my head. I have no idea if Tessa's saying anything about me—or who she's saying it to—but I know my mouth is shut tight. I try not to watch her for more than two seconds at a time. She's not pretty, really, but she's not ugly. She has lots of muscles, and she's strong and confident, like Derek. I would even say she's a little sexy, though I would never say that out loud.

Tessa catches me stealing a look at her, and her eyes light up. I look away as fast as I can and spend the rest of the night studying Derek's ass. It's a nice one. Not as nice as Rob's, but nice.

Hers is out of the question. I don't even know what it looks like.

You have a quiet and unobtrusive nature.

Asian Sensations, Los Angeles

Today my job is to take bruised apples out of the apple display. Easy enough, except I keep dropping them because Rob is ordering salad dressing on the other side of the produce section, and his lovely bippy is facing toward me. I would love to pat it. Not hit it, not grab it, just pat it. Maybe I'll walk by and brush it, and then I could claim it was an accident. "Oh, sorry, Rob, just trying to get by." He might believe me.

It's suppertime on Friday night and the place is humming. People are streaming in by twos and threes, grabbing stuff for weekend barbecues and fiestas, and any second someone's going to call me up front to check. I'm trying to make sure my apples are decently stacked before that happens when Tessa comes rolling up the aisle with a full shopping cart, and that's odd. Most people start with the fruit and veggie aisle because it's closest to the door, but not her.

I try to disappear under the heap of fruit, but it doesn't happen before she sees me.

"Hi, Morgan." People are milling around grabbing strawberries and oranges, and she's in their way, scooping pears into a plastic bag. Everyone's giving her dirty looks.

"Hey." I keep my eyes on the apples. I hear a woman mumble under her breath as she reaches around Tessa for a pear.

"So … how are you?" Now she's pretending to find the perfect plum.

"Fine. How are you?" My eyes don't leave the heaps of red.

"Uh … fine. Seeya." And she beats feet out of the produce aisle. Not soon enough for me.

I try to relax my brain by taking Rob in again. He's got on his white button-down shirt and black pants with the appropriate green apron over all of it, so I can't see any other tattoos, but I've decided he must have one on his stomach somewhere.

He looks up as I go by on my way to find a box for the bruised apples. "What's the hurry? Wanna help me order salad dressing?"

"What? Uh … I need to go get something." I skitter into the back room, hands shaking and clammy. I was going to brush his ass, then I was practically invited to do so, and I turned him down.

The next time I go to the side of the valley, the first thing I will shout is, *I AM SWEARING OFF KISSING FOREVER.*

Your dearest wish will come true.

Chinese on the Green, Atlanta

I borrow the car again from Grandma and drive out to my hill. She never tells anyone. I scream *I AM A BIG FAT ZERO*, plus *I AM SWEARING OFF KISSING FOREVER*, and *I HATE BEING A SECRET SEX FIEND* and *YOU SUCK THE RIGHTEOUS TIT* about sixteen times each. I found that last one on the side of a building in Omaha when I was there for mock trial. It's really good for anger. After I scream I roll around in hysterics on the ground, then I try to pick the grass out of my hair. Then I sit very still and watch a hawk swirl over the fields.

My mind is on Grandma as I drive back into town. She lives at 120 W. 11th Street, Central Nowhere, and she is my secret weapon for sanity. I love her to death, and not just because of her Amazon account, with which she will buy me almost any book I ask for. She is definitely the reason why I love words. And we have the same birthday—she says I was the premiere gift for her fifty-first, and the best present she's gotten in her whole life. Right.

She is strange and cool in lots of ways. She belongs to

Nebraskans for Peace and she's been married three times, which is very odd for a grandma from Central Nowhere. But she also was a concert pianist, which is not your usual occupation, and she started when she was twenty, she was that good, so if I'm going to live up to her creative legend I'd better get my writing ass in gear. She played a lot with the Omaha Symphony, which you wouldn't think was such a great symphony since it's in Nowhere, but they've won all sorts of awards. Plus she did a lot of solo work and contracts with other orchestras, so she's been all over the world as well as to all fifty states.

I always hated it when she was gone. She used to drive to Omaha almost every week for rehearsal, which is almost five hundred miles round trip, and she'd be gone for weeks at a time when she went on tour. Even though she retired a few years ago, she still plays a concert here and there. And she has this fantastic fortune collection from all those gigs. She said she always ate at least one Chinese meal when she was on the road, and then she'd write the city on the fortune she got. How cool is that?

We both liked the color pink when I was little, and she still does. Plus, she's very witty. On the door to her garage, she has a Post-It note tacked to the frame right at her eye level. All it says is "Teeth? Hair!" I think it's the funniest note in the entire universe. She's my dad's mother, and she's the sanest person in my biological crowd.

She calls me Morgan le Fay, like the high priestess of Avalon. She likes to claim I'm named after that Morgan, but I'm sure I'm not. My mom and dad weren't that imaginative.

Grandma tells me I get my powers of language and my beauty from Morgan le Fay, but I tell her I got those things from her.

It's not like she doesn't love my brothers, Martin and Evan, because she does, and they love her back. And she'd probably loan the car to Martin, too, if he were old enough to drive it. But she's MY grandma. Mine. And I'm hers.

I park the car in her garage and go inside. She's making us tea because she saw me drive in, and she gives me a big smooch on the cheek. "Hello, doll baby. Did you have a nice shout-out on the hill?" She told me she used to holler crazy things when she was on tour for a long time, but she'd go into a bathroom to do it, since there weren't thirty-mile-wide river valleys to use.

I give her a hug in reply and a big kiss on her cheek. "As a matter of fact, I did. But let's cut to the chase: could we use your Amazon account? I'm jonesing for a new book." My grandma reads more than anyone I know (not just music), and she's not afraid of computers even though she didn't grow up with them.

"And what might you be hankering after?"

"How about *Howl*?" I like the Beats, but mostly the poetry. The Great American Novel from them was *On the Road*, but Kerouac is too arrogant and egotistical for me.

"Your wish is my command. But I'm not touching the computer until you come sit. Using my car without sitting and chatting is unacceptable!"

We drink tea and laugh for a while, then we order the

book and I walk home. Being with her is the easiest thing in the world.

If I were truly a sorceress, like the real Morgan, I'd zap the two of us right out of here. We'd go live by the ocean and read a book a day. We can both do that—read a whole book in a day, a long book, too. My personal best was 425 pages until the seventh Harry Potter came out. Then it was 756 pages in twelve hours, which won me the Nerd of the Century Award.

I might zap Rob away, too, just for his cute ass. If he reads, that is.

Simplicity and clarity should be your theme in dress.

Yellow River Phoenix, Washington D.C.

School started today. The phone rings while I'm sitting on the couch at home, air conditioning turned down to negative seven since it's still August, trying to absorb the fact that I have to start thinking again from eight to three every day. My books almost oozed out of my hands while I walked home.

"Morgan!" says the voice on the phone.

"What? Who is this?"

"You don't know?"

"Um ... no."

"It's Tessa! Geez!" She sounds disappointed.

I look out the window to see her standing in her kitchen, waving at me. She could open her back door and holler and I'd be able to hear her just as well.

When we were in sixth grade, before the social hierarchy started (which was also the year her family moved into that house), we were close. We laughed and talked through every single class we had together, and when it was warm, we'd sleep in one of our back yards and do the same thing. Our parents would get pissed because we'd keep them awake if the windows were open. It's still safe to sleep in your back yard in Central Nowhere.

But in middle school, the social ladder started growing rungs. I stayed down with my books, and she and her party tendencies went up. Even so, she'd call me late at night, which thrilled my parents to no end. Sometimes she'd say her brothers had smacked her around. Her mom and dad seem okay, but she has two older brothers who like to use her as a hockey puck when they get angry. She'd say, "Why, Morgan? Why was I born into this family?" I never had an answer.

Sometimes when Tessa was really upset she'd go on about suicide. This happened about once a month, and I really don't like to admit this, but I got used to it. When you're in eighth grade, you don't get how serious it is when someone says they want to kill themselves.

Her sniffles would be loud. "Would anyone care?"

"I'd care. I'd miss you. Your folks would miss you."

"My folks don't give a shit."

"Sure they do."

"But you'd miss me?" There was always hope in her voice.

"Who else would I laugh with?"

"I have the gun right here."

I have no idea if she had a gun, but she said it every time. And I should have told someone, but I never did.

"Put the gun away. Don't tempt yourself."

"Why don't you come over here and stop me?"

"Because it's eleven thirty at night and my parents won't understand when they catch me sneaking out. Put the gun away and go to bed. You don't want to die."

"You'd really miss me?"

"Yes. Now go to sleep. Okay?"

"Okay. I love you. Good night."

"See you in P.E."

And that would be that. Until the next time.

She always said she loved me.

Beware of trips down memory lane.

"Morgan!"

I'm still back in eighth grade. "What?"

"Can I bring over the ACT books my mom bought me?"

"Right now?"

I look out the window again and she holds up a couple thick books, so I hang up and wave her over.

We meet up in the back yard, and she rambles on about last Friday night, the volleyball game this Friday night, Evie Munson's pregnancy, and Ethan Johnson's pot bust, which puts a serious damper on the football team's chances this year. I page through the books and give her a few "uh huh" noises to let her know I'm there. This chatty thing is weird, especially after the shy treatment in the produce aisle, but I let her keep talking.

I wonder if her brothers still beat her. Amazingly, that's one thing my dad doesn't do. More than once he's said to me, "Well, at least I don't hit you." Like it excuses him.

But hitting leaves bruises, which are (1) easier to see, and (2) harder to deny. He's not willing to go there.

"Are you listening?" She bonks me on the arm.

"Oh … yeah."

"Now that we have books, I suppose we should actually study sometime."

"If you want."

"I don't want. But I might as well." She picks up her books and heads across my grass to her grass while she waves over her shoulder. "Gotta get the stars in alignment to buy some Wild Turkey. Seeya!"

Wild Turkey. Gross.

I go inside for some Post-Its and a pen, then I write.

For lasting peace, sit in the back yard at least once a day.

Beware of big fat books bearing study questions for college exams.

Watch out for neighbors bearing Wild Turkey.

I stick one Post-It on the grill, one on the air conditioner, and one on the door into the garage. We'll see if anyone notices.

Versatility is one of your outstanding traits.

The Ginkgo Tree, Helena

It's study hall, and we've been in school for a month. It's still hot out there. When I went to lunch I saw a kid with his brains sagging out of his eye sockets, but at least they weren't dripping on the ground. All the popular girls are still wearing shirts with maximum cleavage. Doesn't this school have a dress code?

Do something useful, even if you're sweating your ass off.

I am doing my best to engage my brain, but all that's floating through it are words like *zygote*, *obfuscate*, and *flummox*—words I'll never use in conversation. When I was in eighth grade, I got a note that said "Dear Morgan, you walking dictionary," signed by about twelve girls in my class. I don't know if anyone else remembers that note, but I do.

Mr. Solomon picks his nose, very carefully behind his book so he thinks we can't see him. He sniffs and goes back to reading, which is what I'm supposed to be doing, but I'm watching him instead. He looks up and sees me checking him out, so I grin and he scowls. Solomon doesn't like me. He doesn't like anyone, actually—he likes British literature, and only dead British authors at that. But Mrs. Koch likes me. She was my English teacher last year, and she teaches Great American Novels, stuff like *The Sun Also Rises* and *Beloved* and *The Great Gatsby*. She doesn't mind that I use big words, or bug her about how to make my literary mark on the universe.

School is one of the most annoying experiences on the planet.

I write it on a piece of notebook paper, crumple it into a ball, and loft it toward the back of the room. Solomon misses the entire thing because he's picking his nose and reading again.

Tessa walks by in the hall, deep in conversation with Amber Sibley, and they're waving their hands at each other and scowling. I have no idea what the topic of conversation might be, but better Amber than me.

I corral my brain into thinking about homework so I don't have to take it home, and my brain settles into a hum that does not include words like *ubiquitous* or *megalomaniac*. For an hour, I think about what's on the desk in front of me and nothing else. It's a nice change of pace.

When the bell rings, I bolt for the door just like everyone else. I find my locker, pack up my crap, and try to walk home without liquefying.

The house is cool and dark. Perfect. I stretch out on the living room floor and flip on *Oprah*. Brain candy is good for everyone, even walking dictionaries like me.

And then everyone comes home, all at once.

Try not to throw a fit when your space is invaded and you're minding your own business, having a cookie.

Here's the general nightly routine in my house. Any time between 4:15 and 6:00 p.m., my father walks in the door and hightails it down to the basement and the laundry room to put his beer in the "beverage fridge," as he calls it. He says he brings home the beer so he can relax, and he does relax: into a mean, angry puddle. I was thirteen before I found out that everyone's dad didn't bring home a case of beer each night. And he doesn't buy it at my grocery store, either—he goes to a liquor store. He must think we don't know how much he drinks. And what does he drink? Old Milwaukee. For volume drinkers, it's the best bargain.

Before he comes back upstairs to greet us, he stands next to the dryer and cracks one to chug. Then he brings another one upstairs and greets whoever's around.

"Hi, Morgan."

"Hi, Dad."

"Where are your brothers?"

"In their rooms."

"How was your day today?"

"Fine. How was yours?"

"Fine, thank you." No challenge or confrontation on weeknights, because the drinking starts too late in the day. He reserves the tough stuff for the weekend, when drinking starts at noon.

My stepmom Anne is completely sober but dangerous as well. She's an elementary school teacher, so she usually gets home not long after me. She has her evening routine, too. She fixes supper, then tries to blend into the woodwork, no different than the rest of us. Her best defense is her piercing Look of Doom, which she lays on us kids but never on my dad. And he deserves it more than we do.

Nine-year-old Evan, my halfway bio bro, gets home with Anne. He's in third grade, but he's not your average third grader. The other day I caught him talking to a light pole. When I asked him why, he told me he didn't know, but inanimate objects need love too. You can't argue with that. As a family member, he's a good choice—his mother, I don't know, but I had to get her to get him. Evan stays out of my way and is nice to me most of the time. I can't ask for much more.

Martin, my fully bio bro, gets home at various times. He's fourteen and has a job, so sometimes he's here, sometimes he's stopped at his friend Brian's house to play guitar, or sometimes he's just...off somewhere else. Once he's home, he's invisible. If I want to see him, I sit on his bed and watch him polish his acoustic guitar. It's beautiful. Dad and Anne don't know he paid $1,250 for it, a fortune to save at his age. He wants to be the next Hank Williams—not Hank Williams, Jr., but the original. It's unique, I'll give him that, and I suppose no stranger than wanting to write the Great American Novel. Or fortunes.

On most days, suppertime is its own circle of hell. A traditional dinner-table conversation:

Dad: "So, Anne, how was your day?"

Anne: "Fine. And yours?"

Dad: "Fine. Anyone have a big day?"

Morgan, Martin, Evan, in unison: "No."

Sometimes under my breath I mutter, "Hell, no." When Anne hears that, she says, "Morgan, remember your audience. Are you winning friends with curse words?" I don't want to be friends with anyone in this house, except sometimes Martin and Evan. The three of us bolt our food down as fast as we can.

By seven o'clock, supper is over. Dad's in his recliner in the basement family room (where we are never a family, so it should be renamed "the drinking room") slugging back more brew and reading the magazines stacked ankle-deep around his chair. By nine, he's passed out and snoring away. Anne has faded into the living room (not the family room, where Dad is) with a book. Martin is in his room with his guitar, Evan goes to bed early, and I go to my room and write. Usually it's opening lines for novels, things like *Once upon a time a man named François lived in an outhouse*, or *Bees never fly in straight lines*, or *The first night I leave this town I'm going to get a tattoo of a smiley face on my ass because I'm so happy to be gone*. Sometimes I get a few paragraphs to go with my opening lines. But not often.

Today Dad is home early, for some reason, and everybody else is more or less on time. I retreat to the back yard, even though it's still hot out. My fortunes are still stuck to the grill, the AC, and the door to the garage. Underneath

> Watch out for neighbors bearing Wild Turkey

someone wrote,

> Watch out for wild turkeys! They'll attack you!

Supper is especially silent. I'd judge my dad to be on his fifth beer or so. He's not slurring his words at all, but his eyes are beady. That's not a good sign.

"Morgan, how was your day?"

"Fine, thanks, Dad."

Anne chimes in. "Morgan, how's school going? How do you like being a junior?"

"It's fine."

"Martin, how about you? How's freshman life?"

"Just fine, thank you." Martin glares into his plate. But at least he remembered his manners and said "thank you." If he hadn't, it would have brought a tirade about how impolite children are these days, blah blah blah.

Her smile looks forced, but Anne continues. "Do you and Morgan ever see each other at school? Is it hard to find your way around?" This is Martin's first year at the high school.

Martin continues to speak to his peas. "Well, yeah, we see each other in the hall, and I can find my classes."

All of a sudden Dad clears his throat. "I … uh … have an announcement to make."

Anne looks like she wishes she could crawl under the table. Martin, Evan, and I just stare.

"I'm … uh … changing jobs."

Nobody says a word.

My dad manages—managed—a car dealership, so I was hoping he could get me a deal on a car. But with what I make at Food Freak, it would've been ten years before I had enough.

"Well, Brad, that's . . . unexpected." Anne has to gulp a couple times to get out that last word. "Did you just hatch that plan, or have you been thinking about it for a while?"

"I . . . uh . . . just thought of it today, actually. Or . . . well, Dave thought of it for me." Dave is his boss. Was his boss.

"I see. Well, we can talk about this later." She stands up and takes her plate to the sink, then grabs her purse and heads out the door. We hear her car drive away.

Silence. The three of us look at each other. Dad looks at us looking at each other.

"Do you kids have anything to say?"

I can't help myself, because I have cramps—that one particular kind of cramps—and I'm tired, so I feel like ripping into someone. "Smooth move, Brad. Is this the first time you've been fired?"

His hand comes up from his lap and his arm moves back, gathering force to strike. But then it stops, hangs in midair for a second, and falls back into his lap. His eyes never leave mine. The force of his rage blasts at me from every pore.

"Ungrateful. Rude. Bitch."

It's the worst insult he can muster—I've heard him say it to Anne, too. It's not bad, but it's not the best he could do if he thought a little while.

Now it's my turn to stand up. I don't look at him. "Do

your toxic brain cells prevent you from coming up with something else? You use that one too much."

I gather Evan and Martin's plates and put them in the dishwasher along with mine and Anne's. When I look at them, Evan and Martin are frozen in place.

I wave my hand in the direction of their rooms. "I'd hide, if I were you."

They immediately evaporate. I throw the leftovers into some plastic dishes and slam lids on the containers while Dad stalks downstairs to his beer fridge and his stacks of magazines. His dishes remain on the table.

Not a single word passes between any of us for the rest of the night. Anne still isn't home when I go to bed at ten. If I was older I might be able to understand why she sticks with a guy who has beer and cigarette breath, not to mention coffee breath in the morning, and gets fired. I might even understand what could make someone an alcoholic. But I doubt it.

When I get to my room and settle in with my notebook, I get about three sentences written, thanks to the screeching in my brain. Can you be sixteen and write a memoir? I want to write one called *My Life as a Disco Ball.* Everything reflects off you and you're removed from the fray, up near the ceiling, twirling away.

For lasting peace, remain alone for the rest of your life.

I write it in large letters on a piece of red construction paper and hang it on the door to my room. It's much more polite than *STAY OUT, ASSHOLES.*

Anne came back about one that next morning. I'd given up trying to sleep and was in the back yard—of course. I heard the door slam, then I heard yelling and dishes breaking. I have no idea if Evan and Martin slept through it.

When I was listening to the progression of the fight in my house, I was watching Tessa's place, because the same thing was going on in her house. Lights blinked on and off as the fight moved around her house. Finally someone came flying out the back door and flung themselves onto the ground. The shadow sobbed loud enough to wake up anyone who'd slept through either fight. Then I saw the flicker of a cell phone. After a few more minutes, a car pulled up in front of Tessa's house and another figure came around the corner. It helped the figure on the grass stand up, and then they walked back toward the car.

The second shadow was definitely a girl, so odds were high that the first shadow was Tessa. And the sobs sounded familiar.

I stayed out for a few more minutes, then snuck in to

bed. The entire house was silent. When I walked by the living room, I noticed Anne was asleep on the couch. The sheet she'd grabbed from the closet had slipped off everything but her feet, so I draped it over her.

I didn't fall asleep until after I heard Dad open the front door and grab the morning paper, and I slept until supper. They believed me when I said I was sick.

You are very expressive and positive
in word, act, and feeling.

Wok the Wong Way, Kansas City

It's study hall again. Caitlin Hanson, a senior girl, motions me over to her desk. I go, just because I'm feeling polite, but something's wrong. In the history of the world, Caitlin has never talked to me. Her social status doesn't allow for idle chitchat with nobodies.

She's conspiratorial. "You live behind Tessa, right?"

"So?"

"Could you get us some photos of her and Amanda in bed? We'd pay you."

It must be my face, because Caitlin laughs. "You could sneak over at night. Do you have a digital camera?"

For some reason, I hear that question even though my brain is still trying to process her request. "No."

"You can borrow one of ours. What do you say?"

"Why do you want digital pictures of Tessa and Amanda?" My hands are clammy again.

"Amanda's a cheerleader, right?" Caitlin leans close. "We want to put up a website and get her kicked off the team."

"Oh."

"So will you do it?"

"No."

"Are you a lezzie, too? Is this a conspiracy between you and Tessa to convert as many girls as you can?" Caitlin is hissing.

"No. But I'm not gonna spy for you."

"I said we'd pay you!"

"I've got other stuff to do." I go back to my desk.

When the bell rings, Caitlin whispers "lezzie" as she goes by me on the way out the door. I throw a pencil at her back.

Stick it up your ass.

I write this on a piece of notebook paper, stick in into the vents of some freshman's locker, and stomp home. I think I've already used that one, but so what? If it's a bad day at the fortune factory, I'll use it again and again.

You will soon have many bright days.

Emperor's Wok, Boston

Facing is how you fancy up a grocery store, and lately I have been doing lots of it. It's not a difficult activity—all you do is pull the cans and boxes to the front of the shelf and stack things in neat rows, to make the face of the aisle look nice. When you're done, it looks great, like very busy fairies have invaded your store. But it also looks like no one's bought anything. Is that what management really wants? My hands are big, so I always knock things off the shelves. But facing makes time go fast. That's a plus.

Sometimes food packages say very strange things. The other day I was facing cereal and saw "Enlarged to show texture" on the front of one box. Don't you think people will know pieces of cereal aren't six inches across? Last week I found a can that said, "Contents may explode under pressure." That seemed more relevant, though no less obvious. But anything will do that. Not just Spam.

Rob and I face Aisle 10 for most of our shift. It sounds slightly dirty when you say it like that, "face Aisle 10." Rob's not much better at it than I am, because his hands are big, too. Aisle 10 is the baby aisle, so we are doing our best not to knock off those tiny jars. Baby food explodes when it hits the tile and it's hell to clean up. Glass and creamed spinach go everywhere.

Megan, this sophomore, comes by at some point to ask Rob about whether or not she should do the peanut-butter-and-jelly backstock. If she flirts any harder she'll hurt herself. Rob seems amused, but I'm not. She flounces away again, ready to tackle the Smuckers, and I give her the finger as she goes. Rob doesn't see.

He picks up where he left off, turning labels out to face us. "What are you doing after high school?"

"College. Duh."

"Not going to hang at the Gas & Ass?" He gives me a sideways glance with a smirk attached to it.

"No, thank you. I've had enough of the G&A."

"Oh, come on. Your boyfriend hangs out there all the time."

"How do you know who my boyfriend is?" Now I give him the sideways glance. And then I linger too long. He is *sexy, beautiful, fine, good-looking, stunning, striking, handsome, bodacious,* and *bitchrod.* His hair is sun-kissed, wavy, and slightly longish, plus he's tan and he's got that ass and those arms. I'm still dying to see what his stomach looks like. Washboard, I'd bet, and I hope his tattoo is right at the spot where his stomach muscles fade into that flat plane of pelvis, just above his thighs, and if I don't stop thinking about his body I'm going to have to go stand by the freezer backstock. In the freezer.

Rob laughs. "How do I know? It's a small town, I've only been out of school for a year, and it's also not like you two have been dating for a week. Second, I've seen you with him."

"Where?"

"Oh, like when he drops you off at work?" He snorts.

My hands are a little unsteady with the jars of fruit. "Back to the original point: my parents would freak if I didn't go to college."

He knocks off a jar of baby applesauce but catches it. "Does it matter what your parents think?"

"They're paying, and I want out of here, so yeah, it does."

"Nice to have a funding source."

I try not to drop a jar of peaches. "Is that why you didn't go?"

"No."

"Why not, then?"

"I'm too stupid." He keeps turning labels.

I give him an elbow. "You're stupid for saying that! And you can't be an exchange student if you're stupid."

"How do you know?"

"I asked somebody." And then I blush, because a grin spreads across his face like molasses, slow but steady, and I realize what it means that I asked somebody.

Rob reaches for a box of rice cereal. "So you're asking around about me?"

"No."

Nobody says anything for a minute. I knock off a jar of bananas but catch it.

"New topic: tell me what's so great about writing." He keeps straightening boxes.

"You don't give a crap about writing."

He's surprised. "Sure I do. I read."

"You do?" Good news on that front.

"Duh. What do you want to write about?"

"Anything. Whatever goes in the Great American Novel."

He shifts the last box of rice cereal into its spot. "So where are you going to college? Somewhere you can experience the events in a Great American Novel?"

I turn a can of formula around. "Anywhere but Central Nowhere."

He smiles. "Another duh. Big school or little?"

"Big. So I can blend in. Maybe in a city for a while."

He climbs onto a milk crate so he can reach the back of the top shelf. "Too many buildings."

"Manhattan has more interesting stuff than the entire Midwest."

"How would you know?"

"I went with my grandma once, when I was twelve. When she played at Carnegie Hall."

That gets his attention. "Carnegie Hall?"

"She's a concert pianist."

"Impressive. So what did you see?" Rob is lining up jars of pears.

"A dude ice skating with his reflection at Rockefeller Center."

"No you didn't."

"He was looking in the windows next to the rink, skating with his reflection and having a great time."

"See? Too many crazy people in Manhattan." Rob rolls his eyes.

"Oh, whatever. You're just jealous."

Boxes of oatmeal, Rob's next project, tumble off the shelf and he picks them up. "Cities are full of muggers, rapists, trash, piss, and noise."

I blow dust at him from the tops of the formula cans. "See? You're negative as well as jealous."

"Probably. But cities are shitholes."

"So you want to live here for the rest of your life?" The jar of apple-ham cobbler I'm moving migrates into the line of beef-pea paste because I'm paying more attention to Rob than to my task. I move it back to its home. Baby food has some weird mixes.

"Remember the cows? I'm saving for a ranch."

"Talk about a dead-end career!"

Rob's face was boarded up in an instant. "It's what I want to do, thank you very much. Like you know anything about it."

"Well, nothing but debt in that career."

"My dad's doing okay, Little Miss Cynicism."

I pull the bottle brushes and packages of nipples to the front of their hooks. "So why aren't you working full-time with him? Isn't that what most country kids do?"

"He wants me to have a fallback career. Don't forget, I'm the assistant manager here."

"Of what? Goofing off?"

"Watch your mouth, Morgan." But I see his smile.

Now I line up the carrots, but my lines are getting wigglier instead of straighter. "Can a person really make a career of groceries?"

"Probably." He frowns. "Do you know how much a loan is to buy a ranch? About thirty years' worth of working four jobs."

"It can't be that bad."

His face is cloudy. "You live at home, so what do you know about bills?"

"Does paying bills have to suck the fun out of life?"

Three jars of carrots threaten to jump ship. Rob pushes them back. "Whatever."

"So go work on a ranch, then buy it in a few years." I bring all the packages of baby wipes to the front of the shelf. "Do something bold. You're nineteen, not ninety."

"I've been out of the country. That's pretty bold."

I bat my eyelashes. "Yeah, but now you hang out in a grocery store and talk to underage girls." I bat again, for emphasis.

He focuses on the sippy cups. "I like working here, especially when I work with you. I like working with my dad, and I like having enough money to pay my bills. I'm glad to have four jobs. Okay?" He says "okay" the way people do when they want you to shut up.

"Okay." Better to back off than ruin my chances.

We continue to turn labels and line up jars. Nobody says anything for a long time. I finish the shelf I'm on. "Want a soda?"

He grins and wipes his hands on his apron. "Sure. It's almost quitting time. And why do you say 'soda' instead of 'pop'? What kind of pretentious writer girl are you?"

"Don't you think 'soda' sounds better than 'pop'?"

"Why does it matter, as long as you're not thirsty when you're finished?" Rob straightens the last jar, turns and winks at me, and heads toward the break room.

He is so annoying. But so cute.

After school, I walk downtown with Martin because we
both have to work. His spot is The Tool Shed and he does
what I do—stocks shelves, sells people stuff. Not exciting, but it's something to do to pad his Get Out of Town
account. He wants to leave as bad as I do.

Our high school is kind of at the edge of town, but
"the edge of town" is only ten blocks or so from the Tool
Shed and Food For Freaks. Our little spot in Central
Nowhere was built in the 1870s or something like that,
and it's your basic Midwestern small town: one main
intersection with a few more empty storefronts than
stores, and a collection of houses scattered beyond it. For
most of the twentieth century, we also had the advantage
of having Highway 30 run right through us, which goes
from Astoria, Oregon, to Atlantic City, New Jersey, so our
town thrived on all that traffic. Then I-80 was built just
a mile away from us, so traffic got slow on Highway 30
but people still stopped because of the interstate exit. Any
farther away from 80 and the town would have shriveled

up. Things just slowed way down instead, so voilà—our town's narcoleptic instead of dead.

We have a shock-absorber factory that poisons our water supply, alfalfa-drying facilities that smell just like burning pot, lots of stinky cows, and piles of corn. Not a whole lot of anything a teenager would find *interesting, appealing, relevant, entertaining, witty, stimulating,* or *scintillating.* To say the least.

It's nice out today, not hot but not cold. Fall is getting down to business, so the trees look a little sad and scraggly, like Mother Nature's been stealing from them. A couple people have Halloween decorations out. The houses stare as we go by, and I kick some leaves at Martin, just for fun.

"Knock it off, Morgan."

"What up, homey? Why so quiet?"

He's shuffling his feet. "You sound really really stupid when you talk like that."

"Like what?"

"Like some gangsta rappa."

"Just trying it on for size."

"Whatever." He kicks the stick in our path.

"Why so tense, dude?"

No answer. He continues to ponder his shoes.

"Mart, what's your prob?"

His face crumples around the edges, like he might cry.

"Hey!" I grab his arm and stop him. "What happened?"

"Dad."

"Did what?"

"Took away my guitar." He's trying not to sob.

"Your expensive one?" He's got a bunch.

"No, the electric one I won when I kicked Aaron Cousins' ass at the Battle of the Bands." Martin sniffs. "It's a cheap piece of shit, but I still like it. I only had my amp up to seven, and I thought no one else was home." I see a tear on his face.

"Do you know what he did with it?"

"He said he gave it to the Salvation Army truck that was here on Saturday." The Sal comes from Kearney once a month to pick up donations.

I am pissed. "Honest to God?"

Martin swipes at his face. "He didn't. I saw it in the garage yesterday."

Give your brother a helping hand as often as you can.

I laugh. I don't want to hug him on the street because he wouldn't talk to me for a month, so I pat him on the shoulder, then pull him a little. "You need to get to work. Me too."

He nodded. "Gotta clean the back room today. Fucking mess of hammers in there." He wipes his nose with his sleeve. Of course. Gross.

Threatening to give away a kid's guitar—that's cruel.

We walk a ways. "Doin' better now, Mart?"

His mouth is a flat line. "Still pissed."

"Don't blame you. Me too."

And then we're at the hardware store. He goes in and I head to Comida Burrita. *Comida* is "food" *en español*. I looked it up. Maybe I can get Rob to whisper sweet Spanish nothings in my ear—he should be really good at it after his year with Argentinean cows. Maybe he whispered sweet nothings *en español* into some South American hottie's ear. I can see that. But did she whisper back?

Don't fuck with hammers.

Parents suck ass.

When I get to work, I find a roll of cash register paper, the kind receipts print on, and write *Parents suck ass* about twenty times with a black magic marker. Then I drape it over an end cap of Tide and walk away.

You are about to make a most valuable discovery.

The Greek Speak Chinese, Athens

It's snowing outside. I am sitting in Algebra II, watching it snow, on October 19th. Maybe the world's going to have another Ice Age, which would be fab with me. No one would have to worry about what they looked like in a swimsuit, and we'd all have skis and sled dogs. I'd like having sled dogs. But every time I see a flake hit the ground, it melts. It will be a while before the snow sticks for good.

I should get back to the problem on the board, because Mr. Morrison is looking at me like I'm not paying attention. Since I'm not.

I feel a whack on the back of my head, and I turn around ready to yell at Jeff Frederickson, who sits behind me. But it's Tessa. She gives me this conspiratorial smile. What did she do with Jeff?

I scowl. "What is your issue?" I have stayed as clear of her as possible lately, which is difficult when there are only three hundred people in your high school, but I've been working hard at it. And I have not been staring at her house late at night when the lights are off. I have not.

"Just buggin' you. Did you see it's snowing?"

"Where's Jeff?"

"He's not here, so I thought I'd sit behind you. You need something to do."

"I have math to do. Mr. Morrison is gonna yell at us."

"The practice ACT is in two weeks. Should we actually study?"

"I don't know." I really wish she'd leave me alone.

"I'll be over after the volleyball game on Thursday." She gives me a twisted smile. "I have to take Amanda home first." I must have reacted to that statement, because the glare was instant. "What?"

I retreat from her glare. "Nothing! Mr. Morrison is gonna yell if I don't turn around."

"So?"

Just then, we hear a low growl from the front of the room: "Tessa and Morgan, how's the problem going?" I've never met a teacher with that same kind of growl.

"Fine." We say it in unison.

I give Tessa a look before I turn around. "Thanks for pissing him off."

"No problem, girlfriend."

"Don't call me girlfriend!" I say it louder than I want to.

I don't turn around fast enough to miss her expression—she looks like I slapped her. But then she's bonked in the head by a wadded-up piece of paper and she forgets me. Krista Anderson is staring at her with the most intense "please pick it up *right now*" look on her face. Tessa grabs the note off the floor, and I turn around.

On Thursday after the game, Tessa comes over, hauling her big fat books in a backpack. We don't mention Amanda, volleyball, or anything related to anything. Nobody looks at anybody. We do stupid exercises until eleven thirty, when she walks back across my yard to hers, rubbing her arms to keep warm. As she lets herself into her back door, she looks back at my kitchen window. I don't know if she can see me watching her.

Conceptualize. Organize. Then do.

Dragon Wok, Richmond

Rob and I are alone in the laundry aisle. This is one of my favorite hangouts for two reasons: (1) it smells good, and (2) it's on the far side of the store, so no one bugs you except for Megan, she of the saccharine syrup mouth and endless questions about backstock.

We bring the humongous cartons of Tide, All, and Clorox, which are heavy as boxes of boulders, out on a stocker cart. The cart is kind of like a surfboard—long and narrow, but with four-foot-tall handles at each end and one set of wheels in the middle of the cart. It's hard to control but a blast to ride. Once we unload the cartons we move the cart to one end of the aisle, then Rob gets on and I give him a shove. Once you're on, you try to stay on and pray you don't crash into anything.

We surf until we're caught by some crabby customers who threaten to report us to the manager, which is funny, since Rob the manager is the one doing most of the goofing off. We politely say all right, yes ma'am, it won't happen again, and get back to work. I'm sure the whole place hears us laughing.

I'm bent down, tucking some bottles of Tide into the back of a shelf, when I feel something brush my ass, pause slightly, then move on as quickly as it arrived. Kind of like a butterfly and my ass is a flower. Rob's been rambling on about combines—it's harvest time so he's been helping his dad, and harvest is a rather unsexy topic—so the brush is completely unexpected. I'm glad he can't see my face, because it's in flames. I don't say a word, because I'm afraid of what my voice will sound like. Then I hear, "So what about the Huskers for Saturday?"

I slowly bring my face out, being careful not to smack my head on the shelf, and turn to look at him. His face says nothing is different, like he hasn't just befriended my ass. Like he hasn't just given me something to remember on a Friday night with Derek.

I try to sound normal. "No. They're not up to creaming anyone right now."

"We'll see what happens. You never know with the Huskers, especially lately."

"How did we get on the topic of football?" I feel my face cooling off.

"No clue. Care to discuss which laundry detergent is better?" He shoves a box of Clorox down the aisle toward its spot. We shelve it, empty three more cartons of soap, then surf carefully to the back room.

Enjoy the sensual power of laundry soap.

I am a walking nerve ending and a big fat chicken for not cussing him out for touching me. It's my ass, after all. Not that I'm not okay with it, but he shouldn't just assume.

My ass is a flower—what an awful metaphor. I'll be canned at the fortune factory before I start.

Megan, who's up by the checkstand, hollers at me when I walk out the door. "Bye, Morgan!"

I turn and give her a polite smile and a wave. Rob has stopped to talk to her and turns away from my wave, pretending to decide whether he wants a Snickers or Reese's Peanut Butter Cups.

I stomp out the door and cross the parking lot to Gas & Ass. Derek's there, waiting for me, and I watch the door of Food Fineness for Rob to come out while I'm trying to listen to Derek's blah blah. When Rob does come out, I grab Derek and plant the biggest, sexiest kiss on him that I can. Of course Derek loves it, so we get into this serious mash, which I don't break off until long after I'm sure Rob's left.

Take that, Grocery Boy.

Be a smart cookie: look, listen, and hear.

Golden Garden, Cheyenne

Tessa comes through my line today with a box of frozen fried chicken.

"Yum. That for you?" I send it over the scanner: $4.58.

"For my parents. I'm a vegetarian. Well, I try to be." She hands me a five.

I drop the money. "A vegetarian in Central Nowhere? Not possible."

She picks up the bill and hands it to me again. "It was easier once you guys started carrying soy milk and tofu, but I can't do it much during the school year—this athlete needs animal protein." She flexes her arm muscles at me. "But I don't eat this stuff. It's really cut-up pigeons."

I laugh, and she leaves.

Easy as pie. No weirdness. Fine with me.

After work I decide to visit Grandma, even though it's a longish walk from Food Fracas to her place. She has my copy of *Howl*, and she's refused to bring it to my house— I have to come to her. She has a fancy-but-comfortable house on the west side of town, where she's lived for thirty years.

She answers the door in her organ shoes, so I know I interrupted her. She's practicing for a Thanksgiving weekend concert at St. Cecilia's Cathedral in Omaha. She has a hundred-year-old piano and a full-sized church organ in her special music room, which itself is giant-sized, and she can play any song you ask for, in any key, and change the key in her head when she wants to. Her organ shoes are red tie-up numbers, the likes of which I have never seen before except on her feet. They have boxy toes and square heels, not real high, and there are lots of laces. Sort of organ-playing grandma hooker shoes—sedate but oddly sexy.

"It's you, Morgan Elsie Callahan! Come in, come in. I was just playing the organ."

"Hiya, Elsie Yvonne Callahan. How are you?" We give each other a kiss and walk back to the music room. Even though she's had three husbands, she never changed her name after the first one because she got famous as a pianist using Elsie Callahan. Her second husband's last name was Smith, boring, and her third husband's last name was Wennerschmacht, which is hard to say, let alone spell. I'm just glad her last name matches mine.

"What are you playing?" I lie down on the floor, hands under my head, and stretch out. I took piano lessons until last year, so I am fairly knowledgeable about classical music. But I don't care if Grandma plays Aerosmith, 50

Cent, or Beethoven—I just love to listen. She is the most talented person I know.

"It's called 'Requiem for a Lost Girl.'"

"Who wrote it?"

"I did." She sits back down on the organ bench and gets re-prepared, shaking her hands and flexing her ankles. While she plays the keys with her hands, she plays the pedals underneath the organ with her feet. The pedals below are their own keyboard, bigger than the regular one but with the same black and white keys. I couldn't be that coordinated in nine thousand years.

"I didn't know you wrote music."

"Just this song." She shakes her hands again and takes a deep breath.

BOOM! An enormous G chord. When the piece starts, I close my eyes. It's slow, full of a kind of sorrow I don't know and hope never to know. But it's also complicated and intricate, like Bach without his joy. And she plays with the enthusiasm of a kid let loose in a toy store, no matter how sad the music is. I love that. She's the goddess, not me.

When she's done, she swivels around and looks at me. She is built solid, like a fortress. Sometimes I look at her and think, "That's me in fifty years," because I look just like she did when she was a girl. Now she sort of looks like a female Colonel Sanders. I don't want to look like a man when I'm sixty-seven, but too bad.

"Morgan."

"What?"

"What's wrong with you?"

"Why do you ask?"

She nudges me with her foot. "Morgan le Fay, oh Goddess of Avalon, you don't come in here and lie on the floor. You sit down in the chair and pester me with questions until I can't stand to play anymore. This time you listened. What's wrong?"

"Nothing." I try not to fidget. That always gives me away.

"Don't lie to me. Remember, I'm your grandmother and your birthday twin. You can't lie to a birthday twin." She taps her toe, like she's waiting for a bus.

"I'm not lying!"

"You are, or you'd be looking me in the face."

She has me there. I had my face covered so she couldn't see my eyes. She always looks in my eyes.

I get up off the floor and go sit in the chair by the organ. She stays on the bench.

"I hate my life." Which isn't really true, but it's a place to start, and it sounds like something a girl who's sixteen would say.

She is unfazed by this declaration, since I've made it before. "You can't hate your life. There's nothing to hate."

"Ha! Have you tried living my life?"

"No. But you're young, and you have so much left to do that what's going on now will be peanuts compared to the rest of it." Grandma pats my hand, which is not condescension on her part, just comfort.

"It doesn't make today suck any less."

"I can understand that. But I also know that today doesn't really suck. You're just talking like a sixteen-year-old." Her smile is kind.

We're silent for a bit. She's good at being quiet and letting me think.

Now I really confess. "How do you know, Grandma, what's love and what's just sex?"

Do not assume your grandma is a square.

She almost falls off her organ bench because she laughs so hard she cries, and I have to get her a Kleenex. Then she snorts, and that cracks her up even more. She finally settles down enough to talk again. "Is that what your worry is?"

"It may not be serious to you, but it's damn serious to me."

"Don't curse, sweetheart. And I don't mean to laugh at you. I'm laughing at the seriousness of your question, and the fact that you're *asking* the question at sixteen. There's a time and place for that question, and it's called college." Her guffaws have settled into chuckles.

"It's right in front of me, so I'm worrying about it."

"Then I can see why it's on your mind." Her face is serious, but her eyes are still full of laughter.

"So what's love and what's just sex?"

"I can't help you there, sweetheart. I've only had sex with three men in my life, and that was for love each time. My generation does things much differently. Duh."

Duh? Now I laugh. Grandma and slang don't mix very will.

"Honey, why does this matter right now?"

"Because it does."

"Why the love part? Why not just the sex part?" She grins.

"Are you really my grandma? What did you do with my grandma?"

"I ask because I want to know what you think love means."

"Is it different at sixteen than it is at sixty-seven?"

She pats me again. "Well, darling, yes. Yes it is. And you can't know that until you're here at sixty-seven. But I want to know what it is for you, so I can see your side of it."

"Okay. Well. Love is . . . someone to be close to. Someone who will take care of you, and care about what you're doing. Care that you're happy or sad. Care enough to make you laugh, or ask how your day was." Derek flashes through my mind. So does Rob. My dad and stepmom flash through next, with a big red NOT circle over the top of them. Then Evan and Martin, but the NOT symbol isn't there. Then Tessa's face floats through.

"At sixteen you should be able to get that stuff from your parents and your friends. You shouldn't have to get it from a boyfriend."

"You know as well as I do that my parents are otherwise occupied, to put it delicately." Grandma knows how her son loves the beer fridge. She also knows how unhappy he and Anne are.

Her face is sad. "I know, sweetie. I'm trying to love you."

"You do a good job, but it's different with guys. You

know that. I have *such* a crush on this guy I work with. And then there's Derek, and then there's a girl at school who sort of seems to like me, at least she might, and she … "

Not even Grandma can know about the back yard.

"A girl? This is new information." The laughter is back in her eyes.

"Well, I'm not exactly sure. Rumor is she's a lesbian, and I think she might like me."

"Does that bother you?" It doesn't look like it bothers Grandma.

"No. Maybe. Yes." Now I've really got the fidgets.

"Why?" She's as calm as I am nervous.

"Why should I have to be liked by a girl?"

She gives me another kind smile. "It's a compliment to be liked by anyone. And uncross your arms. This isn't a crabby situation."

Maybe it is and maybe it isn't. But I don't say that.

"Here's my thought, granddaughter. Stand back, take things slowly, and let it all happen the way it will. Don't worry about love *or* sex. Worry about getting good grades. Worry about your brothers. Let love take care of itself. And tell your crush and your boyfriend to keep their bassoons in their cases."

Now it's my turn to snort.

She laughs, too. "Isn't that silly? Our conductor used to say it to the men on tour, and he always told the women to leave their maracas in their bags. That's not nearly as good as the bassoon comment."

I look down. "I've never thought of my breasts as maracas." They're not bad maracas, at any rate.

"Honey, I love you. I want you to be all right." Despite the smile, this time I see the worry in her eyes.

"I know. I love you, too."

She shuts the music on the organ. "Want to hear about my latest read? It's not quite the next Great American Novel, but it's good. It's on the table in the living room, if you'll go get it for me, right next to *Howl.*"

She was the person I gave my first story to, when I was ten. She told me it was great, like any grandma would, and then she told me how I could make it better. That's what got me: she took me seriously. Like I was a real writer. I will never forget it.

Before I grab her book and mine, I go sit next to her on the organ bench and she gives me a big grandma hug— her special version, made from strong arms, old-fashioned perfume, and years of practice. The kind that makes you think you've won the best prize in the world.

For love and safety, find your grandma.

You are not a person who can be ignored.

Red Moon Ocean, Omaha

It's been at least two weeks since the ass-touching/kissing-in-the-parking-lot evening. Nobody will be doing the outside kissing thing for a while, though, because it's freezing out there now. I hate November. But it's warm in the Grocery Garden. Rob and I are stocking the paper part of the soap aisle. TP, paper towels, and napkins are fun to stock because they're so light, and you can pitch them from one end of the aisle to the other and no one gets hurt, unless a customer walks through the battle. It's not as great as stock-cart surfing, but it's fun.

Rob and I pitch TP at each other for a while, then we set up paper towel rolls like bowling pins. We sneak over to the juice aisle and grab a big can of V8, then bowl it down the aisle as fast as we can. Paper towels fly everywhere. Then Boss Man Steve calls, because he's gone home for supper but forgot to tell Rob something, so I pick up the backstock that's scattered from one end of the aisle to the other. Crazy Gus comes by and tells me what a nice sculpture it is and I have no idea what to say, so I thank him while he wobbles off.

Then it's my turn to take a break, so I head to the break room—if you can call a table stuck next to the time clock a break room—after I buy a can of soda. I drink it while I watch the hands go around the time clock. I don't smoke, so I don't have anything to do on break but go pee and drink a soda. Exciting.

"*¿Chica bonita, donde estás?*" I hear Rob's voice in the back room somewhere. He must have gotten in through another door, because he didn't pass by me to get back there. Our back room is enormous, with at least six doors. You could drive a semi in there.

I have no idea where he is or what he said. "Can't see you, but I can hear you."

"Do you know where the toothpicks are?"

"What are you, helpless?"

"Seriously. I could use another set of eyes."

I find Rob and his voice. He's buried in the stacks of boxes, so I look in the stacks, too. The toothpicks are right in front, a little box among the big ones. Before I can turn and say, "Hey, weirdo, they're right here," Rob brushes my ass again. With both hands. Gently. But with pressure. Less like a butterfly, more like a human.

Be careful of hotties searching for toothpicks.

I always thought it was made up, that a person's legs could do that rubbery thing, but it's all I can do to stand up. I command my legs to hold me, and I whirl around to face him.

"What the hell do you think you're doing? This is the second time you've touched me without permission. Do you think my ass is a toy?" I give him my stern face.

"No." His head is hung low.

"Then what? I am not a plaything."

"I know. I just want you to know I like you." He sounds like a little kid.

I try to look grouchy, even though my heart is doing strange things. He's so cute, standing there with his muscle-y arms and sweet face, looking like he's twelve. "You have a voice. So tell me."

"I like you." I can barely hear him when he says it.

"Okay then."

"Okay."

"Don't touch my ass again. Unless I say you can."

"Okay." He reaches behind me, picks up the toothpick box, and heads back to the soap aisle without meeting my eyes.

He can't do that, put his hands wherever he wants. He should ask first. All that aside, I'm still a noodle, and I have trouble walking back up front. Crazy Gus wanders into my checkstand, slipping ramen and radishes on the belt. Then, from somewhere, he produces a loaf of bread—but it's rye, so he's not branching out as much as I thought. I get his grimy self and his groceries out the door, and I realize I've stopped being a noodle. Sort of. My stomach feels funny, but it's not tickly weird funny. It's stomach-won't-stop-heaving funny coupled with oh-my-god-that's-hilarious funny.

Rob likes me. I like him. There's Derek. And we can't forget Tessa.

My break is definitely over.

You are always welcome in any gathering.

Buddha's Pearl, San Diego

All of a sudden, the rumor that Frosting Girl is a lesbian is everywhere right now. Who started it, I don't know, but my bet is Caitlin Cheerleader Bitch Hanson decided to get revenge since I wouldn't take photos.

Of course Derek wants to discuss it. We couldn't have Mr. Handsome Football Player Doofus with a lesbian girl-friend, now could we?

He comes to pick me up so we can drive around, since all there is to do in this town is drive around. We have no teen center, we have no underage bars, we have one movie theater that isn't open right now because it's four in the afternoon, we have no Target, we have nothing to do but waste gas. And with gas prices, we can't even drive around very long. So he cuts to the chase.

"I need to ask you something." He's tapping his hands on the steering wheel, jittering around and looking like he'd rather be anywhere but here.

"What?" I know what's coming. I heard the rumor

today in Mr. Solomon's class. Jessica told me while Solomon was explaining *Bleak House*.

"I've heard things about Tessa. And you. Together." Jitter jitter.

"From who?"

"My friends."

"Like they're a good source. What did they say?"

"That you two were hugging and kissing at a football game."

An average teenage guy has the brain power of a raisin.

I roll my eyes. "Two women, kissing at a football game, in this town. Where do you think we are, California? Good lord!"

He stops jittering and gives me a hard stare. "So is there a reason to believe them?"

"What do you think? You've known me for two years. Am I a lesbian?" I glare. But inside, my brain is spinning. Maybe he's the one who knows the answer, given our weekend wrestling sessions. Maybe it's me, not him.

"Well…" Now he's driving past Gas & Ass, grinning and waving at his buds getting out of their cars. My store floats by on the other side of the G&A parking lot.

I smack his arm, hard, because I can't stand to be blown off. "I am your *girlfriend*, asshole. Of those two years, I have been having sex with you for one of them!" It took me a while to give in, and for what? I shouldn't have bothered.

He sighs, focusing on the road again. "You don't always seem to enjoy it."

Who knew he was paying attention?

I cross my arms. "Do you think I'd have sex with you if I wanted to do it with girls instead?"

More hand twitches. "I don't know. Would you?"

"You are so freaking dense!" I'm really starting to holler. "Why should you believe the rumors anyway?"

He tries to reach for my hand. "Can you blame me for asking?"

"Yeah, I can. Tessa and I are friends! Not even close friends."

Then he grins. "Thinking about you two together…"

Never underestimate the power of pornography.

I almost spit at him, I'm so angry. "Take me home. Now."

And he does. The closer we get to my house, the angrier he gets, too. By the time we get there, the frostiness inside the car matches the temperature outside. When I get out of his car I can't slam the door hard enough, and he squeals his tires when he pulls away.

You will make many changes before settling satisfactorily.

Hong Kong Fong's, Nashville

Derek isn't speaking to me. It's been six days.

The day after Derek and I had our fight, the phone rang.

"So what did you say about us?"

"Who is this?"

"Derek actually yelled at me."

I finally recognized the voice. "He did? Why?"

"He wants to make sure you are who you say you are."

I looked through my window and saw her in her kitchen, with her back to me. "Uh ... yeah."

"I told him there was nothing to worry about."

"Well ... thanks." I tried not to breathe my sigh of relief into the phone. But if she thinks I'm straight, why did she kiss me?

She hung up and I stared at the phone. That conversation was the weirdest I've had in a long time.

We have such a cozy love rhombus: Tessa's sticking up for me, Rob is brushing my ass, Derek isn't talking to me, and I'm still trying to figure everything out. Something. Nothing. Anything.

You can have your cake and eat it too.

Fashionable Pearl, New Orleans

I swiped a fortune cookie from the deli today.

You can have your cake and eat it, too.

Here's my response:

If you eat your cake, you'll have a big ass.

Word.

Retirement does not mean quitting life.

Speedy Wok, Sacramento

It's lunchtime, and Martin and I are standing by the pop machine. Whoops—soda machine.

"Are you going to work after school?" He's punching up a Pepsi. He loves to drink it in thirty seconds, then burp the beginning of the Gettysburg Address. Whenever I think I've hit my weirdness zenith, he tops me.

"Yes, much to my dismay." His Pepsi is stuck somewhere in the machine so I give it my best hip-check, which works every time. The machine coughs it up.

"That's fantastic! You should do that more often. Maybe you'd get free—hey!" A hand grabs his shoulder.

"Check it out, Martin. Did you know you were living with someone like her? A crotch-muncher?" I look up, and this crowd of junior and senior girls is bearing down on us. Caitlin Hanson is in the middle, articulating each and every syllable with her hand still on Martin.

I throw my algebra book at them, which is bad because I'll have to go pick it up, and of course I miss everyone, so it makes a decent-sized thunk when it hits the floor. And it's not like they're really an "everyone." They're Caitlin, Dana Combs, Maddy Shepherd, Katie Marshall, and Piper Franzen. They all looked shocked and back up a little.

"You don't want to do that again. What if I tell someone?" Caitlin scoffs and walks away, her posse trailing behind.

Martin looks at me, more than confused. "What's a crotch-muncher?"

"Same thing as a carpet-muncher. See you after school." I retrieve my book and storm into algebra. I write *People in high school are mean, nasty, unkind, cruel, malicious, despicable, unpleasant, uncaring, ruthless, wicked, callous, hateful, malevolent, unkind, spiteful,* and *horrid* all over the book cover, at least five times.

If and when someone in this school—or this town—actually admits they're gay or bi or anything else besides straight, I have no idea what will happen. Everyone claims they're all about family values in Republican states like this one, but that's only as long as your family and your values are just like everyone else's. If they're not, well, tough shit for you and watch your back. In the early 1990s, three people in a small town in Eastern Nowhere killed a girl who passed as a guy. They said he betrayed them. Granted, it's a surprise when Brandon turns out to be Teena, but is it reason enough to murder someone? In this state it is.

I will admit the stereotypes have been fun to listen to. Some examples:

- A lesbian has short, spiky hair. That's how we discovered Tessa, after all. *Right.*
- A lesbian wears combat boots. *So does any woman who owns Doc Martens.*

- A lesbian smokes cigars. *Yuck.*
- A lesbian drives a truck for a living. *At least you'd get to go somewhere.*

It's amazing to me that people are so dumb. I honestly don't blame Tessa for staying in the closet.

After algebra I see Derek, and we just glare. But by the time I get done with work, he's waiting for me at G&A. He opens the door and looks at me. I get in, but I make sure my body language is frosty cold.

The car is silent for a long time. We've never been on the outs for this long. He tries to hold my hand and pull me closer to him, but I stay on my side of the car and make my hand all limp and wimpy so it's no fun to hold it.

"Hey?" His tone is gentle, but I'm not buying it.

"What?" I stare straight ahead.

"I'm sorry."

"Oh." I keep staring.

"I should have known better."

I finally look at him. "You know the truth—you *live* the truth with me." A little voice in my head says, "Does he really?" but I ignore it.

"I know."

We don't say anything for a while, just drive around and look at the lights in people's windows. When I finally let him hold my hand, he cradles it like it might break. His face is soft and he keeps giving me sideways glances. Maybe he's expecting I'll Jackie Chan his ass, I don't know. Before I get out at my house, he holds me close for a long time. I don't tell him so, but it's nice.

> The road to knowledge begins
> with the turn of the page.
>
> Golden Palace, St. Louis

Today in study hall I opt for a field trip to the library, because I'm supposed to be doing research for my English class—for a paper about John Donne, of all people, who is so not a Great American Novelist—and Derek's in the corner with a bunch of friends. They're making paper triangle footballs and shooting them through each other's fingers.

I can't pretend I don't see him, because the book I need is behind their table, so I smile. "Hey, Derek."

"Hey, sweet thing! What are you doing in here?"

"Research for my John Donne paper."

"Come sit." He pats the chair next to him.

> Laziness is doing nothing constructively.

I sit, and he immediately starts kissing my neck and working his way up my face. His buds go back to the paper footballs.

I push him away. "This is the library!"

"So?"

"What if we get caught?"

"What are they gonna do? Kick us out? Big loss." He starts with the kisses again.

"It would be for me."

"You are such a prude!"

Derek's friend Mike checks me out. "So, Morgan, I hear you like girls. I'll give you a Benjamin if you and Tessa do it in front of me."

Derek says nothing. So I blow. "Mike, I charge two grand to let people watch, and Tessa charges another two grand. Your Benjamin doesn't touch it." I turn and push Derek, hard, in the chest, then whack Mike in the back of the head with a book and push a chair into their table so hard it falls over. But everybody looks at them, not me. "You assholes have a nice day."

Sometimes the rage just descends on me. Maybe that's not good.

I go back to study hall because I don't know what else to do, and I fume until the bell rings. I trudge off toward Grocery Fiesta after school, and about three blocks from school I see Amanda. Of all people. She's walking toward me, so I can't avoid her.

I'm polite. "Hey, Amanda."

She stops in the middle of the sidewalk, hands on hips. "Is it true?"

"Is what true?" I brace myself.

She's pissed. "About you and Tessa? You're a couple now?"

"Why would we be a couple now?"

What does she know?

Amanda slaps me, hard, and I stagger backward. "She's mine! Get your stinking bisexual hands off her!"

She storms away, and I stand stock-still. I can feel my mouth hanging open, so I shut it and walk to work.

Can she see something I can't? Is there a secret signal somewhere, or some chemical signature I don't know about? It was a great kiss, a fantastic kiss. I loved it. I can't deny it. But I've had no desire to kiss her since then. What if I want to kiss some other girl instead? I think Angelina Jolie is smoking hot, so am I a lesbian for saying so? Or am I really bisexual, like Amanda said? Brad Pitt is just as hot as Angelina Jolie, so maybe I want to do it with guys and girls. If those two ever volunteer, I'll take them up on it.

I don't even know how to do it with girls. Nobody ever shows you that part on TV. Well, not on network TV.

I am so inside my head, thinking about what Amanda said, that I walk right by the Grocery Haus. When I'm about a block past it, I realize what I've done, and I hustle my ass back to the store, praying nobody saw me go by the first time. When I walk back by the plate-glass windows, I look at my reflection. I don't think anyone can see Amanda's handprint, but I don't know.

Your kindness to another pays unusual dividends.

Jade Jewel, Austin

It's Thanksgiving break, and I can use it. I am so tired of people looking at me. There's got to be a way to shut people up.

I could give Derek a quickie in the hallway. How would it be any different than what we do on Saturday night, except we'd be standing up?

I could wear a chastity belt. I looked on eBay to see if they had one, and they do, but it's scary-looking. If I wore it on the outside of my clothes, it would shut people up. But I'd be the kind of dork to lose the key.

I could run away. I have enough money saved up from work to buy a bus ticket. But where the hell would I go? I'd worry about Martin and Evan, plus I'd have to start school again someplace else—or get a job instead. But getting a job means no college.

Sudden changes of mind may seem more appropriate than they really are.

I scribble it on a random page of the phone book in red

crayon after I'm done setting the table for our Big Family Feast of Yuckyness.

Our Thanksgiving dinner is a solemn one. Grandma is here, which is great, and Anne serves us a big turkey with all the accompaniments. But Dad still doesn't have a job, and he's on his sixth Old Milwaukee, purchased long before the holiday closed the liquor store. By the time the meal's over, he's passed the twelve-pack mark. Grandma goes home with tears in her eyes, Anne goes to the living room, and the boys go—of course—to their rooms. As my father passes out by himself in the drinking room, I walk out and go to work.

Call it comparison shopping, but I decide to study the women that come through my line. For some reason, there are lots of people at the store on Thanksgiving evening. Maybe everybody ran out of food after fixing Thanksgiving dinner, or maybe they're already sick of turkey. Maybe it was an excuse to get out of the house, with which I am in complete sympathy.

Some of the women are fat old housewives, some are moms dressed up for the holiday, and some are regular single women. Some are women I don't know, so they must be in town to visit relatives.

I check out boobs and asses, and I watch them walk around. I think about how round and cozy women are, and I consider kissing each one of them. With lots of tongue. I think about touching them like Derek touches me.

Women are soft, which is not a bad thing, but softness doesn't make my heart go pitter-pat like hardness and muscles do. But Tessa has muscles, too. Maybe she's a happy medium.

Maybe my head will explode in the next ten seconds, so I don't need to think about this stuff.

Then the only female lawyer in town comes through my line. It's sort of amazing we have a female lawyer in Central Nowhere in the first place. She's a divorce lawyer, and I've heard all sorts of things about the men she's put into poverty with her killer settlements. She's got long wavy blonde hair, perfect makeup, and a beautiful body inside a gorgeous blue suit with very high heels. Her smile is lovely when she says hello to me, so I check her out as I check her out. Her name is Abigail.

She unloads the rest of her cart as I'm scanning her items. When she finishes, she looks me square in the eye.

"Why are you staring at me that way?"

I freeze. "What way?"

"Like you're...checking me out. No pun intended." Her look is a cross between annoyed and flattered.

"Um...didn't realize...sorry." I watch the groceries from that point on.

She pays with a credit card, and as I hand her the slip to sign, I brush her hand. Not on purpose, but it's a useful test. Nothing happens: no electricity, no urge, no butterflies, and I'm relieved as hell when she leaves. Good thing she's over thirty and probably doesn't start rumors.

I sweep, to pass the time, in and around the checkstands. Swish, swish, swish. Then I hear, "Hey, I need some service over here."

Of course. Some subconscious part of Tessa's brain sensed that my brain has spent the last two hours entertaining the idea of sex with women.

I scan her box of Banquet chicken. "No Thanksgiving dinner at your house? And I thought you said this was cut-up pigeons and you didn't eat it."

She laughs. "I lied. And pigeons need to be used somehow. Give the chickens a break."

I sneak a quick glance while I'm getting her change. Her hair is bright orange spikes today. When I give her the money, I touch her hand, just barely. No sparks. No white-hot flame.

I get her chicken in a bag. "Enjoy."

"Oh yes. It beats sawdust with gravy every day." She sails out of the store without a backward glance, which is fine with me.

Sawdust with gravy?

I go back to sweeping checkstands. Rob comes up with a doughnut and a bottle of Mountain Dew. Break time.

He bows to me. "Hello, sunshine, how are you? When did you get here?"

I fake-scowl at him. "Sunshine? I don't think I'm very sunny."

"Looking at you is like sunshine on a summer day." He bows again. "I still like you, by the way. See? I can say it now."

My face gets as red as the Christmas decorations that are out way too early. I ring up his stuff and try to be cool. "Give me your money and get out of here, weirdo."

He hands over his cash, I hand him back his change. Our hands brush, not on purpose, and I feel it to the tips of my toes. He whistles as he heads to the break room.

I think it was just a kiss, that night in my back yard. From a very good kisser, nonetheless, but just a kiss.

One strand of my life has just unknotted itself.

You will soon be crossing the great waters.

Lucky Panda, Tampa

I go to Grandma's, and she's baking Christmas cookies, onion bread, and rye bread. Bread is one of her best things.

"Morgan le Fay! Come on in, dolly. Would you like some tea? The water's hot." She gives me a big smooch on the cheek, and I return the favor.

"I'd love some tea."

She puts her bowl of cookie dough aside. "Why such a long face, my girl? I only seem to see you when there's something wrong."

"That's because your advice is good." I plop myself down at the kitchen table.

"I'm flattered. But can you be cheerful next time?"

"I'll try."

"That's all I ask." Grandma gets out two mugs, a blue one for me and the "Sexy Grandma" one we gave her about five years ago. It matches her organ shoes.

She carries the mugs of hot water to the table, then sits and puts the tea bags in. Her table is overpowered by all the books, magazines, and calendars she has on it, so it's a little hard to find a space for the mugs. She's a one-woman office of twenty. "All right, Morgan. What's wrong?"

"Why did you have three husbands?"

She laughs. "Are you thinking I'm some kind of loose woman?"

"I'm just asking why someone would marry three times."

"Each time I had a husband die, I thought it was better to carry the love we'd had to another person than to give up on love altogether. When your dad's father died so long ago, I was devastated and not ready to be alone. I loved Marvin so much." She fishes out the tea bag from each mug, deposits them on a paper towel, and hands me a steaming cup of tea.

"I wish I would've known him." He died two years before I was born.

She sips her tea. "After a while, I began writing letters to George, because we knew each other from the symphony and I knew he'd just lost his wife, too, so we had something to share. In the middle of the grief, we discovered we had more in common than that. We just clicked, as you kids say."

"That must've been nice."

She sighs, and stirs her tea with a spoon she uncovered from a pile of books. "It was nice, but I knew it wouldn't last. Remember, George was twenty-two years older than me, so I knew he'd die first. After he did, I met Hans after a concert in Omaha, and he became the recipient of all my love. Now that Hans is gone, I give all that love to you, Martin, and Evan." She smiled.

"You don't want a fourth husband?" I blow on my tea. Steam is still curling out of it.

"Heavens, no! I don't have enough time to wash my own socks, let alone someone else's. I should share the men with someone else." Her eyes sparkle.

Now it's my turn to laugh. She tries to look coy as she takes a sip from her "Sexy Grandma" mug.

"But loving us isn't the same as loving men."

"That's true. But as you get older, the details of love don't matter as much. I don't have sex anymore, but that's okay. I'm sixty-seven. Too much effort to shave your legs."

I hoot, and she blushes a tiny bit.

"If you're thinking about sex with any of those boys, or the girl you told me about, it will definitely complicate things. As it should." She fixes me with those wise eyes. "You're too young, Morgan."

She can see I know she's right, and also that it's also too late. She sighs. "What's done is done. Some day you'll want to have kids, and you'll need to pick a good person." She pushes her tea mug away from the edge of the table. "I try to love people in general more than in specific, now. Except for you. I specifically love you." She blows me a kiss and sets off a cascade of paper.

I catch most of the stuff and hand it back. "Loving people in general would be hard. Too many buttheads."

Grandma gets up to check the bread. "Old women have lots of time to put love into the world. That's why there ARE old women, in my opinion. The rye bread I'm baking is for the women at church, and the cookies are for the elementary school."

"Who's the onion bread for?"

"You, of course."

"Fantastico!"

"I thought you'd think so." She pulls loaf pans out of the oven. "You haven't been by to borrow the car lately. Are you feeling calm?"

"Not really, but it's cold on the hill! I'm keeping it all inside until spring."

The bread is turned onto cooling racks. "Are you sure that's good for you?" She gives me her concerned face. "Do you feel a need to run around inside my house and shout?"

I ponder this idea. "Could I?"

"Sure." She sits back in her chair and steels herself for the noise. "As long as you don't use curse words."

"I promise to be good. Are you sure you're ready for this?"

"Fire away."

So I do. I try to keep my voice below scream level, but I holler *YOU SUCK* and *SCHOOL SUCKS* and *MY PARENTS SUCK* about twenty times, and *I THINK CLASSICAL MUSIC SUCKS* for Grandma's amusement, and she laughs because she knows I'm lying. I leave out *I AM A SECRET SEX FIEND*. I even roll around on the carpet, which is soft and fluffy and much nicer than the hard ground. Plus there's nothing to pick out of your hair when you're finished.

When I'm exhausted, I sit down at the kitchen table again. My face is red and I'm sweaty, because it takes lots of energy to shout like that. Grandma's not staring at me like I'm crazy or even unbalanced. She's just smiling.

"Thank you for letting me do that. You rock." I hold up my hand for a high five, and she slaps it.

"No, sweetheart, you rock."

"We both rock."

"We certainly do."

> *The only way to have a friend is to be one.*
>
> Hong Kong Pearl, Salt Lake City

Derek wants to go to a girls' basketball game, and I'm not doing anything, so I go, too. Tessa, of course, is all over the court, shooting and passing and fast-breaking it to a 50–34 win for the Central Nowhere Fighting Cougars.

When the game's over and the team's shaking hands with the defeated Wild Warriors, she notices me in the stands and gives me her biggest, best smile and a little wave. I don't smile or wave back, which is pretty mean of me, but Derek's sitting right there and I don't want to get things all stirred up again, with him or anyone else. Then Caitlin Hanson, Ms. Cheerleader-Study-Hall-Spy-Bitch, goes over to Tessa to congratulate her. They act like they're best buds from way back, talking and grinning and punching each other on the shoulder. Caitlin's flipping her skirt at Tessa and Tessa's laughing along, and the wheels of my brain start turning.

I'm not sure I want to know.

There's nothing like good food,
good wine, and a good mate.

Chinese Cuisine, Mobile

The traditional Christmas-present opening is at our house this year, and the *diffidence, coldness, aloofness, detachment, reserve, remoteness,* and *distance* between us is too obvious. Grandma is in one corner of the room, and Dad is in the opposite corner doing his best not to look at her. Anne is plying us with homemade cinnamon rolls plus fancy coffee for the grown-ups and OJ for the kids, so she's flitting from person to person, chipper as a Christmas elf. Nobody's taking her up on the cheerfulness. Martin, Evan, and I are dutifully plowing through the gifts, saying "thank you" and smiling on cue.

But then I open the box from Grandma, and nestled in the tissue paper is a digital camera. Ever since Caitlin asked me if I had one, I've been secretly wishing. Not to take pictures of Tessa. Just to have.

"Thank you so much!" I fling my arms around Grandma's neck and squeeze her, then complete the gesture with a smooch.

She laughs. "I figure you'll be building websites next,

some place to show off your fortunes and the progress of your Great American Novel. What if you want pictures, too?" She untangles herself from my arms. "It's not the world's most expensive camera, just so you know."

"It doesn't matter. Thank you. You're the absolute best, Birthday Twin."

"No, you are."

When I move back to sit in my chair, I see how everyone else reacted to our scene. Dad is sitting across the room from Anne, and they're both frowning and looking at the floor like we were doing something indecent. Martin looks like he wants to hit someone. Evan is taking it all in.

It's not my fault Grandma and I love each other.

I spend the rest of the day taking photos of Christmas-present craziness and lots of weird still-life scenarios. Piles of boxes. My hand. The table after we'd finished Christmas dinner.

Weird, obscure art is better than no art at all.

Grandma catches me taking photos of the after-dinner table. "Is it really worth it?"

"Just documenting."

"Be sure you put the people in. It's the people who matter, not the stuff."

"Come here, then."

She shakes her head. "I look like something the cat dragged in."

Only my grandma would know that the correct word is *dragged*, not *drug*.

"You are beautiful, and you matter. Come on." I lead her into the living room and sit her down in the softest chair. She settles in with a sigh.

"If you want a photo, take it now." She smiles the kindest, softest smile in the world. I click a few. I will print them and put them in my room, to remind me that, somewhere in the world, someone is not insane.

"Thanks, Grandma ol' pal, ol' birthday buddy. I love you."

"I love you, too, honey. Merry Christmas."

"Merry Christmas."

I hug her again and she hugs me back. Her hugs are presents I can get any time.

Whenever my dad gets deep into the beer fridge, he claims Grandma is an evil bitch. He claims she did horrible things to him when he was a kid, like slap him in the face with a spatula so you could see the outlines of the spatula holes on his cheek. When he's really tanked, he raves on about the family secret and how he'll tell me one day when I'm old enough to know, blah blah blah. Like there's a family secret. Like I care.

Generally speaking, dads can be full of shit.

Good news will come to you by mail.

Cantonese Blossom, Seattle

Today is my birthday, and Grandma's. Seventeen (or sixty-eight, for her), with nowhere to go but out of here. Big freaking whoopee. There are some perks to having a birthday five days after Christmas—no school to mess up your fun—but it's a drag not to have presents any other time of the year. And this year I have to work at Bag 'O Fun & Food. Gross. But it's more money for my life after Central Nowhere. It's an early shift, nine to two, and the store is empty, which is nice, but Rob is visiting his cousins in Lincoln so there's no one to talk to.

When I get home from work, I find two envelopes on my bed. Neither has a return address, but both are post-marked Central Nowhere.

The first card is plain but pretty, with "Happy Birthday" on the outside. Inside it says, "You deserve the best." On the bottom of the card is a note: "Hi! I like you! Let's have a real date. I'll call you when I get home from Lincoln. Rob."

I have to sit down—literally—because my legs are doing that wobbly thing again.

It's about time he made his move—you'd think he was a turtle.

How does he know my birthday is today?

I should run this by Derek. See if he's okay with it.

Or not.

After about fifteen minutes of imagining all sorts of things and waiting for my legs to firm up, I pick up the other envelope. I open it and find a handmade card. On the outside it says, "You're the most beautiful thing in the universe," with some nice flowers. Inside, it says "Happy Birthday, Gorgeous." It isn't signed.

I call Derek right away.

"Hey, thanks for the birthday card! Why didn't you sign it?"

"I didn't send anything. I've got yours right here, for tonight."

"Oh." My mind freezes up. "Well...it must be from Ingrid or Jessica or something. I got a card that wasn't signed and I figured it was from you."

"Nope."

Gulp.

"Okay, well, I'll see you tonight." I hope the cheeriness covers the surprise.

"You got it, sugar buns." If he only knew who'd been touching his sugar buns.

I have a guess who sent that card.

Before I go out with Derek, Martin gives me a dictionary. In the front he's written "Happy Birthday, you walking dictionary." I have to laugh. It's big and heavy and makes a fabulous THUMP when you drop it on the floor, so I spend some time doing that. My dad's down in the drinking room, right beneath my bedroom, and he finally hollers, "Whoever the hell is making that noise, just quit that shit!" I hear him through the floor, but I drop it one last time. For emphasis.

Derek and I have supper at Reginald's, the only nice restaurant in town, and we have prime rib. I am such a carnivore. He's even invited Grandma, so the three of us have a grand time. Then Grandma goes home and we go to a movie. I'd been hoping for a nice artistic exploration of the inner lives of madmen, but this is Central Nowhere, so it's an action flick. Then we have two hours left until curfew, and Derek has a gleam in his eye.

"Where to now? Our street?" I give Derek a big sigh. Bad sex isn't what I want for a birthday present.

"Better than that." He looks pleased with himself.

"Really?"

"Wait and find out."

Derek drives me to his sister Bette's house. She's single, so she's almost always gone. The place is dark.

"A surprise party?"

"Kind of."

We get out of the car and Derek lets us in, then covers my eyes while he leads me through the house. Finally he stops me. "Hold still and keep 'em covered. I gotta do something."

I hear him rustling around, and then I hear a bunch

of quiet *flicks*. The darkness behind my hands gets a little brighter.

"Okay, open your eyes!"

We're in Bette's bedroom. There's a vase of roses, and candles all around the room. The covers are turned back on her bed.

Even dumb men can be smart sometimes.

"Happy booty call!" Derek's grin is enormous. As he comes over and puts his arms around me, I try to pretend he didn't just say "booty call." I count the roses over his shoulder—seventeen.

He caresses my face and looks into my eyes, really looks. "I want to make love to you the right way. In a bed. In a house. Happy birthday, sweetheart."

"Where'd you get the idea?" Against my will, almost, I nibble his ear.

"I Googled 'how to make love to a woman.' Good plan, huh?" He's nuzzling my neck.

Booty calls and Google. Of course. Rob is in my mind's eye for a split second. Then I am instantly ashamed, so I pull Derek closer and nibble some more so I don't see his face and he can't see mine. "What a great gift. Thank you."

I don't deserve this.

Derek kisses me. It's a long, slow, deep, incredible kiss. We lie down on the bed and kiss for a long, long time. Then we get down to business.

I don't think about anybody but me. Derek goes slow. And I love it. For the first time.

Listen not to vain words of empty tongue.

China River, Jerusalem

For my birthday, Grandma gave me a stack of ten Great American Novels, so I'm trying to begin one. I've narrowed it down to *Fear and Loathing in Las Vegas*, *To Kill a Mockingbird*, and *The Old Man and the Sea*. I don't feel in the mood for racial tension or weird minimalism, so I pick drug runs through the desert. But I'm not concentrating very well.

I've decided I like the word *planet* a lot. It's a solid word, a useful word. I like thinking of humanity spinning through space on our *planet*, this big ball of water and rock under our feet. But here's a paradox—we all occupy this *planet* and depend on each other for making the *planet* work, yet we're all alone, each of us stuck inside our head.

I have no idea why I'm thinking about this right now. Probably because I'm grounded and it's New Year's Eve and I have nothing else to do. Derek and I blew curfew last night because we fell asleep in Bette's bed and I was an hour late. He's out with his buds, but he calls every hour or so. He would have wanted to go parking anyway, and

I'm not sure I could have gone back to a car so soon. I'm still too blown away by the luxury of a bed. So I comfort him, watch movies, and think about being seventeen.

Only three more years before twenty. Thirteen more years before thirty. I can't imagine twenty, let alone thirty. For my thirtieth birthday I'll have a book signing at some big bookstore in Manhattan, and people will ask me to write things like "with love to Esmeralda" in their copies of my Great American Novel. I'll be the Young Hot Novelist for the mid-millennium. How's that for a celebration?

I wonder how old Morgan le Fay was when she got powerful.

Maybe I've already had my powerful days.

Maybe they're just beginning.

You are the center of every group's attention.

Spring Roll Palace, Memphis

Christmas break: lovely. School again: gross. And through some monstrously unkind twist of fate, Tessa and I have a study hall together this semester. People have started saying we planned it.

Life will kick you in the ass whenever it can.

I am writing it on the bottom of my backpack in permanent green marker when she comes in. "Hey, girlfriend! How was your break?"

I scowl and start heaving books onto my desk. Why do I have so much to do already? And WHY does she keep calling me girlfriend?

Finally I look up. "It was okay. How was yours?" I saw her standing in her back yard a couple times, smoking a cigarette and staring at my house. I haven't said anything about the birthday card.

"Why are you writing on your backpack?" She's trying not to laugh.

"None of your business." Then I see her face, and I stare.

Tessa points to her eye. "Like it?" It looks like someone took a bat to it.

"Which one of your brothers did that?" I can't keep the shock out of my voice.

"Brett."

"Did you call the cops? Where were your folks?"

She makes a face. "In Mexico. No one gives a shit about my eye."

"You know that's not true!"

"Isn't it, Morgan? Do *you* care?" She looks at me with more force than it took to make that black eye.

I shake my finger at her, like someone's mom, and try to ignore what's behind that look. "You could have called me." I can't believe I said it, but I don't take it back.

She sneers. "I'll try to remember that."

"Seriously. You shouldn't be a punching bag for your brothers."

Tessa glares at me like I insulted her. I start my chemistry homework, and she traces the graffiti on her desk with her pencil. After fifteen minutes I can't help looking at her.

"Tessa."

"What?" She keeps tracing.

"I don't know ... just ... Tessa."

"Well, what?"

"Nothing." I go back to work.

Tessa stares out the window. Suddenly she grabs my

arm and shakes it, startling me enough that I drop my pencil. "Hey, how was your birthday?"

I dig under my desk to find it. "How did you remember it was my birthday?" Everybody had birthday parties when we were in middle school, but that was ages ago. Then again, I still know hers is September 3rd.

She looks sad for just a second. "I just did, and then I ran into Derek outside the flower shop when he was ordering your roses."

"We had a good date." I try not to blush.

"Did you ... get cards from people?" The hope is obvious in her voice.

"Just from my grandma." I dig in my backpack so she can't see I'm lying. I'm not a very good liar.

"Oh." She goes back to tracing the graffiti.

I do more homework, and Tessa ponders the snow outside the window when she's finished with the graffiti. After what seems like years, study hall is over.

If the idea you had three days ago still looks good,
do it.

Speedy Wok, Jacksonville

Today at Groceries à la Nowhere, work is quiet until Rob shows up. When he walks in, all I can think about is how fine he is. His smile is so bright he looks like he swallowed the sun.

He hollers from the door. "Morgan!"

"How was your Christmas? I haven't seen you forever!" I'm sure I'm grinning like a fool, too.

"Lincoln was great. How was your birthday?"

I barely keep a straight face. "It was fine, thanks."

Do not let people read your mind.

Rob comes closer. "So when are we going out?"

"I don't know."

"How about this Friday?" Now he's standing about a foot away.

"Um..." Derek and I have plans to go to another basketball game. "How about Saturday night?"

"It's a date, then. Pick you up at six?"

"Deal. Want to know where I live?"

He raises an eyebrow. "It's a small town. I know where you live."

He heads into the back room to hang up his jacket and get his apron. I, on the other hand, have to hang on to the counter to keep from swooning.

Ingrid and Jessica come in about ten seconds later. They must've felt the gossip building up. Ingrid tries to pull a cart out from the tangle and not make it sound like a car crash.

I wave. "What's up, women?"

Ingrid kicks the carts. "Shopping for my mom. Jessica decided to come along."

Jessica waves back. "My parents are painting, and they're afraid I'll spill the paint."

Ingrid talks and pulls at the same time "What's wrong with you? You look like you swallowed a bird." She stops yanking, and Jessica tries. A cart reluctantly separates itself from its kin.

It would probably be smart to keep my mouth shut, but I don't. "You'll never guess."

"So tell us!" Jessica pushes the cart over and Ingrid follows.

"I have a date with Rob on Saturday night."

"*What?*" Both of them say it together.

"You heard me."

Ingrid is the practical one. "What are you gonna tell Derek?"

"Can I tell him I'm with you two?"

Jessica pipes up. "Just tell him we went to Kearney or somewhere."

"Nothing stupid, like sleeping with him." Ingrid looks stern.

"Oh, please! We're just hanging out. I'm not ready to tell Derek he's got competition."

Ingrid stays stern. "But he does."

"Yeah, he does." Jessica jumps in.

"Jessica, knock it off." Ingrid gives her a glare.

"Okay, women, you have to go shop. I've got to check." Old Mrs. Anderson is fast approaching with her cart of cat food, cigarettes, and Cheez Doodles (she must have called Crazy Gus). I'm sure she will ask for her *slip*, not her receipt, and I'm glad she doesn't have a gallon of milk in there or we would have to have words about its price. But milk doesn't start with a *C*. Ingrid heads off toward the end cap of flour, Jessica in tow.

Once Mrs. Anderson is gone, it sinks in: *I HAVE A DATE WITH ROB.*

Holy shit.

When I walk out of work, I look in the windows of Gas & Ass where Derek's waiting to pick me up. Rob's shift got over about an hour before mine did and he's standing inside, too, talking to everyone who's standing around, including Derek.

How can he do that, talk to Derek like he's not planning to stick a knife in Derek's back?

How can I do it?

Between that scene and my own guilt, I'm freaking

out, so I start walking home. By block ten it's so cold I can't feel my toes, and my hands are made of ice, but it feels good on my face, which is on fire. Then Derek pulls up next to me and rolls down the window.

"What in the holy hell are you doing? It's January!"

I get in because it's getting hard to walk. My feet are like frozen pieces of meat.

Once I'm buckled up, Derek grabs my hand. "Why didn't you come over to the G&A when you were done? I was waiting for you!"

"The walk sounded good."

"Good? You could've frozen to death!"

"Oh, please. Global warming won't let that happen."

"Stick with the plan next time." He squeezes my fingers, which hurts because everything's starting to thaw.

We're almost there so I don't have much time, but I try anyway. "So … who was at the G&A?"

"Mark, Dave, Grant, Alec, Rob from your store, nobody important."

"Any new gossip?" I stamp my feet to make them wake up.

"Not a bit. Rob says you're fun to work with."

I make the words come out normally. "We joke around a lot."

Then Derek starts babbling on about football play-offs and the Super Bowl, talking with his hands and being loud, and I try to keep up with "yeah" and "oh?" so he thinks I'm listening, but I'm not.

"Hey!"

I jump. "Why are you yelling?"

"Have you heard a thing I've said?" Now he's annoyed.

"Broncos. Chances to make it to the Super Bowl. Two weeks. You, Scott, Rick, Brady, Marc. Super Bowl at Brady's house, his mom makes the best snacks." Not bad.

"You're a million miles away."

"Just thinking." It's a bad habit.

He wiggles his eyebrows at me. "About what?"

"My stupid parents." A total lie.

We're at my house, and Derek pulls into the driveway. "They're assholes." Then he leans over and gives me a big, warm hug.

His shoulders and chest are full of muscles, so it's like being surrounded by the safest, warmest, hardest-but-softest wall you can imagine. I let him hold me, and I rest. I do love this guy, despite everything else. In those warm, brown, kind pools there's a man I don't deserve.

I pull away. "Thanks for the hug."

He pulls me back and kisses me. "It's my job to make you feel better."

I don't call Rob to cancel. I think about it. But I don't.

I am a complete, utter bitch. Not even bitchrod. Just a bitch.

You have an important new business development
shaping up.

Lucky Teahouse, Fairbanks

Here's the synopsis of my Great American Novel. I wrote
it in study hall while trying not to watch Tessa watching
me.

*Once upon a time, there was a girl who lived
in a small town. She dreamed of moving to New
York or San Francisco, the cities at either end of
Interstate 80, the big, wide road that went by her
house. She graduated, spent $2000 on a piece-
of-shit car, packed up all her belongings, and
decided to go east. On her first day in New York,
someone stole all her stuff and all her tires, so she
became a homeless person and panhandled on
Wall Street. Somehow she managed to find soap,
perfume, and makeup, so she remained beautiful. One day a man noticed her and gave her five
bucks because he felt sorry for her. She asked him
to help her invest it, so they bought one share of
Apple stock. Little did they know that the next day*

Apple would release a version of the iPhone that would contact aliens on the moon. They made $57,395 overnight. She moved in with the man after kicking out his wife, and she bought all the black clothes Saks Fifth Avenue had. She went to the New York Public Library and hung out with the staff of the New Yorker all day while the man was on Wall Street. When he came home, she was no longer a secret sex fiend: she was an out-in-the-open sex fiend. The End.

It's not *The Catcher in the Rye*. But it's a start.

Act accordingly.

Lucky Teahouse, Houston

Rob picks me up in a beat-up red truck.

"What happened to your convertible?" He has been known to drive a very cute vintage red convertible to work.

"Too cold. And it's my dad's."

"The farmer?"

He gives me a sideways look. "Even farmers can have convertibles."

"Why does he let you drive it?"

"He doesn't." Rob smiles as I laugh. "What would you like to do?"

Suddenly I'm shy. "I don't know. You're the man, you plan the date."

"I thought you were a feminist."

That comment gets him a whack on the arm. "I am, but the date was your idea."

"No, it was yours. You're too hard to resist." He backs out of the driveway, and the active deception begins. I sink down in the seat in case we pass someone I know.

Resist flattery if you want to keep yourself out of trouble.

From my crunched-up spot, I look out the window. January is dark. I write *resist flattery* in the condensation on the glass where I breathed on it.

"What about Derek?" Rob stares straight ahead.

"What about him?"

"Where did you tell him you were going tonight?"

I doodle on the glass some more. "Out with Ingrid and Jessica."

"What if he sees them somewhere?"

Oops. "I suddenly got sick. I stayed home."

"Won't he check on you?"

Now I'm sweating. "You should take me home. Right now. Turn around."

He does, and we go back to my driveway. Rob reaches over and gives me a shove toward the door. "Bye. See you at work."

I don't move.

"So go already."

I still don't move.

A laugh from the driver's side of the car. "How about North Platte? No one should see us there."

Finally I answer. "Dude, it's your date."

"North Platte it is, then."

And we drive away. I can't believe it, but we drive away.

North Platte is an hour away from Central Nowhere. It's actually in Western Nowhere, and is a bit too country western for me, but that's not relevant at the moment.

Small talk escapes me, so I stare into the blackness going by.

Rob clears his throat. "So why aren't you talking?"

I don't know whether to tell him the truth or not, but I do. "I'm nervous."

"Nothing scary about me."

"Not scary. Just ... different. Maybe you're going to kidnap me. You know, for the ransom. Plus ... "

"Plus what?"

"I'm totally thrilled you asked me out."

"Well, thank goodness. I thought you were gonna tell me you had some incurable disease and six months to live." Rob wipes his brow and shakes off the pretend sweat.

"What if I had?"

"I know what I'd be doing for the next six months." Very casually, like he's been doing it all his life, he reaches out and takes my hand. "I'm glad you said yes."

We hold hands, look at the stars, and laugh about stuff at Groceries A Go Go. Once we make it to North Platte, we see a movie, some stupid comedy, and laugh our asses off some more. After the movie, we whip through a drive-through and head back home.

"How's the writing going?" He chomps his burger.

Nobody really wants to know about your writing.

I swallow. "Well, you know. Fortunes aren't all that difficult."

"But what about the Great American Novel?"

"Are you making fun of me?"

"No." He raises his eyebrows. "Why would I make fun of you?"

I give him the eye. "How do you know about the Great American Novel?"

"You told me, remember?" He nudges me on the shoulder. "When we were facing baby food."

"Oh. Yeah." Then I remember his dream "Have you found a farm to buy yet?"

He rolls his eyes. "Ranch. And get out of here."

"I'm serious. What else have you got to spend your money on?"

"You."

"So that's why you take me to McDonald's?" I jab him with a French fry.

"Ho ho."

"Seriously, why not take out a loan?"

"Seriously, why don't you just not bug me about it?" He's smiling, but I can tell he wants me to shut up. So I do.

We drive in silence for a while, and then I remember something I was pondering while staring at his tattoo as he made a big stack of Charmin at the end of an aisle.

"Did you have a girlfriend in Argentina?"

He startles. "Why do you ask?"

"Just wondering."

"Well...I had a host sister, and we kind of...got along."

I stare out the window again. "Like 'got along' in the

'because-we're-a-family-this-year' way, or in the biblical way?"

"What business is it of yours?" He's laughing now, which surprises me. I figured he'd be pissed.

I draw more designs on the window. "Just wondering ... if you're attached right now." I can't believe this stuff is coming out of my mouth.

"I get letters from her, but I can't see us having a future. She lives five thousand miles away."

"Is it really five thousand miles to Argentina?"

"It's gotta be close. And I can't read her letters very well, because my Spanish is rusty now. So, no. I don't think she's competition for you." He's chuckling.

"That's not what I meant!"

"Methinks the lady doth protest too much." He reaches for my hand again. "It's okay."

"Whatever!"

And then we're at my house. I have no idea how the trip back from North Platte got so short. Rob pulls into the driveway. I start to get out, but he yanks me back in the truck. I sit still while he walks around to my door and opens it with a flourish. I laugh. "Who knew you were a gentleman?"

We walk to my door. Rob shakes my hand, but never drops it when he's done. "Thanks for the nice night. Surprised to get my birthday card?"

I hope the porch light isn't bright enough for him to see how red my face is. "How did you know it was my birthday?"

"Your stepmom picked up a cake that said 'Happy Birthday Morgan' on it."

I take a deep, deep breath. "Thanks for the great time. Let's do it again."

"You can count on that."

Do not expect more than a handshake,
even though you've been dreaming of alternatives.

Then he leans over and kisses me.

It's gentle, nothing insistent. No tongue. I want *so much* to grab his face and really kiss him, like a crazy woman, good and hard, so he knows exactly how I feel. But I don't want to ruin the moment and scare him. Or me.

He walks back to his truck, waves at me over the roof, and gets in. I watch him drive away, then I float inside. Float to my room, then the bathroom, then float my toothbrush over my teeth. Float into bed and dream floaty dreams of hands and stars in the dark sky.

> There is no grief which time
> will not lessen and soften.

Chinese Jewish Deli, New York City

I'm taking photos of more weird still lifes, like Martin's guitar, Evan's stack of graphic novels, and the recycling bin full of beer cans, so I start thinking about what it means for something to be real. *Tangible.* I really dig that word. If something's *tangible*, I can touch it, lick it, hear it, smell it, or see it, and take a photo of it, too. I know it exists.

But with a photo you can make people think anything. One of me and Tessa holding hands, and you'd think we were a couple. A photo of the cleanest corner of the room, and you'd think the whole place was immaculate. But we're not a couple, and right outside the clean corner, the whole place is piled with crap. Deceptive. The photo itself is tangible, but it can capture a lie.

I also like the opposite: *intangible.* Something you can't see. Something you have to take on faith. Maybe something you can't photograph. Feelings are *intangible*, because you can't see a substance called *love* or *hate*. But you can see someone's face when they feel love or hate, and you can see them kiss or kick someone to express that feeling.

My mother is intangible to me. I was just a little under three when she was killed, and Martin was a baby. I was in the accident, too, but my car seat kept me alive. Nobody, and I mean nobody, talks about it. Or her.

I can remember the color of her hair, and her smile, and I have some old photos to look at, but that's it. Nobody will tell me if she was funny or mean or a good mom, or if they miss her or wish she hadn't been killed. Not even Grandma will talk about her. I can only guess she was awful. Maybe I take after her, and people are embarrassed to admit it.

Her name was Melinda.

If tangible people hurt you, there's more chance to make up because they're right in front of you. You can hit them, or hold them and apologize if you're stupid. Those are the kind of people for me: ones I can cry on and go sledding with, not imaginary people who I can't feel, and who can't love me back. Intangible people like my mother aren't even worth a thought. She's tangible in her pictures, but the pictures are a lie since she doesn't exist anymore.

It was a long time ago, and I should get over it.

There's a good chance of an
important encounter soon.

Emerald Garden, Barcelona

We've been so slow at the Food Barn it's torture to work. It's the winter blahs, I know, but February in Central Nowhere is bleak. People still buy groceries, but they're grouchier while they do it.

Rob is supposed to work tonight, and it's the first time I'll see him since our date. I haven't dared call him, and he hasn't called me. I think we're both afraid of Derek. When Rob comes in, I dig around in my checkstand, trying to look like I'm sorting coupons, but he walks right over. Then my hands shake as I move Mrs. Grabowski's tomato to the scale and weigh it. She gives me the evil eye when I give him my attention instead of her groceries.

"How are you?" His face is flushed with the cold and wind and he looks like one of those rugged dudes in a Chap-Stick ad, all messed-up hair and pink cheeks. Adorable.

"I'm good." What a lame answer.

"I need to get my apron. See you in a minute." Rob heads to the break room.

As I'm bagging Mrs. Grabowski's stuff I have an idea.

Devious. Not what you do when you work. But what the hell.

When Mrs. Grabowski is out the door with her bag, I page Megan, Ms. Outrageous Flirt, to come up front. She's stocking soup. When she comes up I try to look desperate. "Would you cover? I really need to pee."

"Hurry up." She's probably wondering where Rob went and plotting the best way to get him alone in the milk cooler. Too bad for her.

I leave her at my register and hot-foot it to the back. Like I figured, Rob's sitting at the break room table, sipping a Mountain Dew and reading the paper.

"Hola, mi chica. What are you doing back here?"

"What did you just say?"

"Just 'hello, my girl.' Is that okay?"

I tug his hand. "Come with me!"

He stands up. "Where are we going?"

I head around the corner, into the big back room full of boxes and overstock. There are places where the boxes are so high you can't see anything or anyone behind them, and that's what I need. Rob follows me, and way in the back, behind SEAS MDSE, also known as seasonal merchandise, I stop him.

His eyes dart between me and the backstock. Maybe he thinks I'm going to pull boxes down on his head. "What the hell could you want back here?"

I take his other hand, so we're facing each other. "Really kiss me. Right now."

"We're supposed to be working!" His laugh is loud. If anybody heard him and comes looking, I'm screwed.

"No one can see us. Hurry up!" In case it's not obvious, I close my eyes and pucker my lips. "Come on! I've got to get back up front."

Nothing. When I open my eyes again, his eyes are huge. "This is work! You don't do that at work!"

Now I'm crabby. "That didn't stop you from brushing my ass. Twice. Double-standard bullshit is *not* all right with me."

"That was a mistake. Now I'm gonna resist you." Rob drops my hand and looks me square in the face. "I want to kiss you someplace other than this smelly back room next to the sleds. This isn't the time." He's more solemn than I've ever seen him.

All at once I'm so embarrassed I can't stand myself. I lock my eyes on the floor. "You're right."

"But you're hilarious to ask." He tries to get me to look at him. "Hey?"

"What?" I study the backstock. The cartons of Corn Flakes say "Stack 3 High," but there are six cartons heaped on top of each other.

"Don't be embarrassed. Would you settle for a hug?"

"That wouldn't be settling."

Rob folds me into him, and we just stand there for a second. It's perfect. Life is perfect.

CLICK.

"Oh shit, I have to clock in!" Rob lets me go and runs around the corner. I hear the time clock go PUNCH.

I figure my pee break has been way too long, but I don't care. Megan wasn't exactly busting her ass with the soup. So I decide to actually pee, since I'm back there already.

Rob is hard at work on an end cap of Cheerios when I go by. It's corny as hell, but I tingle all over when I pass him and he gives me his best aren't-you-cute smile. That hug will last awhile. Megan is pissed, of course, that I've been gone so long, but she can't go find Rob anyway because there are long checkout lines now and she'd have to help up front anyway. Obviously there were more people in the store than I thought.

I stand and think about Derek as I scan cans of lima beans, bags of frozen doughnuts, big fat beef roasts, and cold gallons of milk. Maybe my policy should be "don't ask, don't tell" when it comes to him. Don't ask for trouble, Morgan, and don't tell Derek when it shows up in the form of Rob. It's probably too late about the asking part, because trouble is currently making stacks of Cheerios boxes at the end of Aisle 3. And all I want to do is stack Cheerios, too.

Use the trowel of patience to
dig out the roots of truth.

Hong Kong Chang's, Des Moines

Tessa throws me note in study hall that says, "I'm calling you tonight." I'm betting she'll ask me out. It's the only thing left. Me, Derek, Rob, and Tessa would make a great quadruple date. But Tessa will be pissed when she finds out her date is Derek.

When the phone rings, I grab it before anyone else can.

"What's up?" She never says, "It's Tessa."

"Doing my math."

"I want to know something."

"What's that?" I barely choke it out. Here we go.

She sighs. "Now that I have a decent practice score on the ACT, my mom wants me to be serious about finding a school and she wondered if you'd help me look." We both took a practice test in October, but I don't know what she got. Some kids talked about their scores, but I didn't, and I don't plan to. Too much room for more labels like "walking college entrance exam."

I try not to breathe my relief into the phone. "You really want to go to college?"

She's instantly hostile. "You think I'm too stupid or something?"

"I just... never mind. Sorry."

Another big heavy sigh. "What about after school?"

I run through a bunch of possibilities. "The library?"

"Thursday. I really want this over with." And she hangs up.

The conversation is so much better than I thought it was going to be that I practically sing for the rest of the night. Not even the random shouts from below of "Brad, you're such an asshole" and "Anne, you bitch" can mess it up.

> Worry is the interest you pay
> on trouble before it's due.

Spring Empress, Philadelphia

On Thursday, Tessa comes to my locker after school as I'm hauling a humongous lump of college crap out from underneath everything else. I'd chucked my college stuff into a big bag before I left that morning, and I had no idea I had so many catalogs and brochures. So why don't I have a plan?

She claps me on the back. "Hey, girlfriend!"

I should get over being annoyed about that.

Mrs. Merino, the librarian, is still around but the library is deserted after school, which was my plan when I suggested it. I try not to be seen in public with Tessa. The rumors have been calm lately and I have no desire to stir them up.

We spread out the college info and I start explaining my process, if you can call it that. "So, um ... I start with academics, because ... well, that's my thing."

Tessa makes a face. "I don't care about that. I'll go any-place that isn't here."

"But you want to get better at what you like to do. That's the point of college."

She crosses her arms and leans back in her chair. "That's gonna be hard, since there's nothing I like to do."

"What about a sports scholarship?"

"I'm an average athlete, and nobody cares. I'm only going because I don't want to work at Gas & Ass for the rest of my life."

"But if you don't want to go, why torture yourself?"

"I've gotta get out of here. Or I'll die. Literally." Tessa stirs the catalogs with her hands as she talks. Her hair is red and black spikes today, our school colors. There's a big basketball game this weekend.

I reach over and grab her hand, to get her attention. "Listen..."

"Don't." She yanks away like I'd blistered her.

"I..."

"Just don't!" She rubs her hand and glares at me.

"Sorry." I go on anyway. "Think for a sec: what would be a dream job for you?"

Big pause. "You'd never believe this, but I like to cook." She looks embarrassed, but I see pride under the fluster.

"So look around for a chef's program."

She sneers. "Are you kidding? There's no such thing." The catalogs keep shuffling.

"Two-year colleges have them."

Another smirk. "How do you know? There's no two-year college shit here."

"I heard Ol' Froggy telling someone about two-years. He said they're the place to go if you want to learn a skill."

Froggy is our guidance counselor, Mr. Frederick, and he has big bullfrog eyes. The school makes you visit him when you're a junior, to do "career counseling." Last week, while I spent twenty minutes waiting for my counseling (which didn't tell me a thing), I heard Chuck Matterson tell Froggy, "I want to go to college so I can smoke weed seven days a week." So Froggy steered him to a two-year.

"Are there any two-years around here?"

"I have no idea. But you could look on the web."

She grabs a piece of paper from the pile of catalogs and letters and writes, "chef program" and "tech school" on it. Then she pauses. "Could I really do this?" Tessa's shoulders are so tense she looks like she'll snap if her arms move the wrong way. If you compared the basketball-court Tessa with the college-bound Tessa, you'd think they were two different people.

"I think you could do it just fine." I smile, because she looks so sad, and Tessa actually smiles back. Nobody's mad, nobody's awkward.

Then she stands up, tall and tough again. "Thanks for the help." She walks over to the computers while I gather up my college crap.

It's comforting to know I'm not the only one who has to get out of this place.

Strange new experiences add to your joy of living.

Dragon Man Cuisine, Sydney

I hate Valentine's Day.

First of all, I don't have to work, which entirely pisses me off. I know that's odd, being pissed that I don't have to work, but I'm all lined up for a shift this afternoon and I know Rob's working, but then Megan doesn't have to go to the orthodontist, so she calls and wants her shift back because Rob's working, and what am I supposed to do, because I can't tell her about Rob, and so I'm stuck, and now what?

As sentences go, that's a pretty good one.

Then Dad and Anne give us heart-shaped helium balloons. I mean, how old are we? Can't we get cash or something? But the balloons are kind of cool, in a strange way. They float through the house on the air currents, and we find them all huddled up in one corner like a meeting of Balloons Anonymous. Hi, my name is Heart #1, and I love people too much. Hi, Heart #1. It's okay.

Of course Derek wants to take me out, and I say yes since he's my boyfriend, and it's the Holiday of Love, and we're supposed to do that. We drive around, looking at nothing, talking about nothing, and all of a sudden Derek pulls over. We aren't anywhere special and we haven't used up our allotment of gas, but Derek has a deadly serious look on his face.

"Morgan."

"What?" I'm expecting him to say he has an STD or something, he's that serious.

He pulls me close. "You know how much I love you?"

"Tell me." I bat my eyelashes. I shouldn't let him do this, but I do.

"I love you more than the moon and the stars and the sun. I love you more than all the fish in the oceans and the grains of sand on their beaches."

I give him a kiss. "That's very sweet."

"I want you to be my wife."

Thud. That's the sound of my heart falling out of my body.

I decide on a light approach. "We aren't even grown-ups!"

"I'm serious. "

"I'm seventeen—barely. You're eighteen. We're children." I rock my arms, like I'm rocking a baby.

He's more solemn than I've ever seen him. "I don't care. Promise me."

Now I'm annoyed. "I have so much other stuff to do in my life besides get married!"

"Like what?" Now Derek looks like I've hit him with a Valentine made of bricks. "I've got a future here! My dad's going to give me a company truck and half the business, and we can build our own house wherever we want."

"So what? I've got to go to college, be a writer, and live a life somewhere else besides Central Nowhere." I try to stay with annoyed, but I'm getting closer to steamed.

"I knew it! You *don't* love me, and all those rumors about you and Tessa are true, aren't they?" He screeches away from the curb, not caring that we're sliding on ice.

I can't decide what to do, so I stroke his shoulder, trying to calm him down, trying to be light. "You doofus! It has nothing to do with whether or not I love you. It has to do with living my life."

"I thought I was a part of your life." He says it like a five-year-old boy.

I lean over and smooch his cheek, trying to smooth things out. "Of course you are. But I don't know anything about my future except for big ideas."

"I'll change your mind." He's driving faster and faster.

Now I'm pissed. "You can't do that! And slow down!"

"If I say I will, I will." Derek is the stubbornest person I know. He means it.

We ride home in silence. I forget to give him the teddy bear I bought him—I accidentally left it at my house—because I'm so freaked out that I just run inside. He'd brought me roses—a dozen for Valentine's Day and two for the years we've been dating—and I leave them in his car.

Do not trust undying declarations of love.

Never hitch your star to someone who will live in a small town for the rest of his life.

Be cautious on Valentine's Day. Duh.

When in doubt, go to sleep.

So I try. But it doesn't work very well, and at three in the morning I'm sitting at the kitchen table, staring out the window at Tessa's house. Someone is standing outside her garage—I can barely see a silhouette. Then I see movement from a second silhouette, and that shadow slaps the first one, then runs around the garage toward the street. Right before the shadow rounds the corner of the garage, it triggers a motion-sensor light.

It's Amanda. I should've guessed from the slap.

Once she's gone, I stare at Tessa's shadow. She stands outside the garage for a long time. Then she crosses the alley and starts moving through the snow in my yard, shuffling her feet. I think there's a pattern to what she's doing, but I can't be sure, and sometimes she moves out of my line of sight. I watch until her shadow goes back into her yard and slips inside. Then I go outside to look.

There's a big heart drawn—or shuffled, in this case— in the snow in our back yard, with "TR + MC" inside it. The snow in our back yard hasn't been touched except for some bunny tracks, so she had lots of space to use.

I stare at it for a second, then proceed to destroy it. It turns out that a snow heart about twenty feet in diameter is very hard to mess up in one's slippers. I about freeze my feet off.

Life to you is a dashing and bold adventure.

Cuisine Chinoise, Paris

It's a teacher workshop day, it's noon, and I still haven't taken a shower. The doorbell rings, and for some reason, I think it's okay to answer the door in my scruffy condition.

"Aren't you lovely?" It's Rob.

"What are you doing here?" I try to smile, but my hair looks like I dried it with an eggbeater and I have no bra on.

"Want to go to Kearney with me? My dad's sending me to pick up parts for the cultivator."

"The cultivator?" I lock my arms over my chest.

"It's March 3rd."

I'm confused. "You don't plant on March 3rd. The ground's not thawed."

"Doesn't mean you shouldn't get the cultivator ready." He says it slowly, like I'm a girl who knows nothing about farming, which is pretty much true.

"Do you mind waiting for fifteen minutes?" I hope I can make myself presentable in that amount of time.

He eyes me up and down. "I'm not in a hurry, and I'm not taking you anywhere in that outfit." But he winks.

"Come on in." I stand back from the door.

He rumples my crumpled hair as he goes by. "Nice 'do."

"Who do I have to impress?"

"No one but the rogue visitor."

"Like I was expecting you!"

Rob smiles. "That was my plan."

I speed down the hall, grab some clothes from my dresser, and scramble into the bathroom. Before I turn the water on, I hear Rob talking to Evan.

"Hi, dude. Tell me about this sheet of numbers you have here." Evan writes these long lists of numbers. Sometimes they're just numbers, and sometimes they have a scheme to them. I've told Rob about Evan and his unique activities.

"First, who are you, and what are you doing in my house?" Good point.

"I'm Rob. I'm a friend of your sister's. We work together." He sits down next to Evan.

"Where's my sister?"

"She's in the shower. We're taking a road trip. Now will you tell me about your numbers?"

Evidently this sheet has a scheme to it. "Well, Rob, this number is the integer of this one, and then I divide each number by four, and then I multiply all those numbers by three ... "

I take the fastest shower on record. Today it's a good thing I'm not a fancy girl. Most of the time I feel like a stranger in Girl World, especially compared with the girls around here, who are perfectly put together under penalty of the destruction of their social standing. No one expects me to look like anything spectacular anyway—God knows someone couldn't be smart AND pretty. That would wreck the social hierarchy. My hair is short, my makeup routine is uncomplicated, and I am not fashion-forward. I have a decent rack, but other than that, I'm pretty average.

As I slap on a little mascara, I listen for more numerical conversation. Silence. When I come out of the bathroom, I realize why I haven't heard any more talk—they're both bent over their work. Evan's paper is full of very long, complicated numbers. Rob's sheet is a list of numbers: 1, 2, 3, 4, 5. All written with the numeral and the word.

I try not to laugh. "Ready, Rob? Or do you need to do some more with your numbers?"

"Evan, can Morgan and I go to Kearney now?" He sticks out his hand.

Evan shakes it. "Sure. Thanks for writing numbers with me."

"It was my pleasure, sir." I can tell Rob means it. Evan isn't the most normal person, but he's charming.

I give Evan a kiss on the cheek. "Be good for Martin. Where is he?"

Evan shrugs. "Where is he normally?"

I stand still and listen. The walls are vibrating very subtly, so Martin's amp is pretty low. They only gave his guitar back last week. "If Dad and Anne come home and ask, tell them I'm with Jessica and Ingrid."

No answer. Evan is bent over his numbers again.

"Evan? Okay?"

"'Kay." He's hard to talk to when he's concentrating so hard.

I walk downstairs and knock on Martin's door. "I'm leaving! You're in charge of Evan!" I hear a loud guitar flourish as my answer. Evan's not really any trouble. We just have to be with him in case he does something weird, like try to climb the telephone pole he's talking to.

We take off for the big city—or what passes for one in Central Nowhere, and laugh our asses off at nothing. And we hold hands. He has nice hands, strong hands, big hands. Good-for-holding hands.

Once we get to the tractor supply store, Rob's a different person, very businesslike and stern. He makes sure the bolts the guy brings him are exactly the right size—Rob brought one from the farm to compare. The sales guy goes in the back three times to get the right ones. Then, while we look for the chain his dad needs, he talks forever to the shop guy about tow strength. I didn't know there was such a thing as tow strength, but it turns out you have to get the right strength for your job. If you get the wrong chain, it could snap when someone tries to use it and kill them in the process. Who knew? A different sales guy has to go in the back three more times to get the right weight of chain.

Always be cautious when choosing chain.
If you should ever need to choose chain.

We finally get everything Rob's dad needs and head back to the truck.

I settle in. "I've never seen that side of you."

"You've got to be careful with stuff like that. People could get hurt."

I sigh. "You can hurt my dad all you want to."

"You're kidding, right?" Rob's slightly shocked.

"No. You love your dad, so it's different."

He pulls into traffic. "Doesn't everyone love their dad?"

I'm silent.

"What's wrong with your dad?" Rob glances at me while he threads his way through the cars and trucks. "Stupid traffic." There's way more of it here than at home.

"He's an alcoholic with an ugly mouth. He's an arseholio."

"A what?"

"It's a British curse word."

"Oh." He stares at the road. "Um...I'm sorry? I'm not sure what to say."

"Yeah, well...I'm used to it by now."

"I'll loan you mine for a while."

"Your what?"

"My dad."

This time I reach out and take his hand. Usually it's the other way around. "I haven't even met your dad."

"Sometime you will."

It's the most generous offer I've had for a long time.

We hold hands all the way home, and I actually feel peaceful. Just for the ride, because I know life will show up when we get home. But for those fifty miles, I'm fine.

You will have gold pieces by the bushel.

Mixed Grill Hawaii, Honolulu

Me and the hill haven't done much communing lately and it's finally warm enough to be out there for longer than ten seconds, so I borrow Grandma's car. Today I shout *I AM A SECRET SEX FIEND AND I WANT ROB* about seventeen times, and then I scream *I HATE RUMORS* and *HIGH SCHOOL SUCKS* and *GET ME OUT OF HERE* and *I NEED A MILLION DOLLARS* about ten times each. Then I holler *FUCK* exactly ninety-nine times.

I am still divided about the F-bomb, because it's so overused in our culture. But it still packs a wallop when it's used well. And it's not overused on the hill.

I get back into the car after about half an hour because it's still pretty chilly out there, and I drive back down to Central Nowhere. I always holler on the east side of the road, and when I pull onto the gravel road today from the dirt track I parked on, I notice a red pickup about a quarter mile west. The truck's familiar, but I don't see anyone.

When I park the car in her driveway, I see Grandma through her kitchen window, sitting at her busy table and shuffling through the mile-high stacks. I knock on the glass. When she sees it's me, she smiles.

I go in and already she's fixing tea for us.

"What's new today, honey bunch?"

"Not much. It's still cold on the hill." I give her a kiss on the cheek, and get one from her in return.

"It's only late March. Got a fortune for me?"

I've told her what I want to do for a living. "Let's see…how about 'Life will work out for you'?"

Grandma hands me a cup of tea. "So what does it mean?"

"It doesn't mean much if I keep working at the Grocery Boutique."

We move to the living room and she settles into her armchair. "But what if you become a famous writer?"

"It takes a while to write the Great American Novel." I curl up in the other armchair.

"There's no hurry, remember? You're seventeen." She chuckles. "Whenever it all works out, you just remember your old grandma. And remember what your first words were to me."

"I have no idea."

"We were getting ready to celebrate our birthday—your first, my fifty-second—and when you discovered presents on the table, you wanted them in the worst way. When I let you open them, you realized what they were, and you handed me one and said 'Read a book.' The first words you ever said made a complete sentence."

"That's me. A genius at one."

I'm kidding, but Grandma isn't, and she gives me a serious version of her beautiful smile. "Exactly what I thought. So write away, honey. Write as much as you can."

I reach over and squeeze her hand. "I'll write books for you."

"No, for you. Write the book you want to find, a book that will jump off the shelf at you and leave you so excited you can't stand it. You can do that, honey."

"I hope so."

"I know so." She gets up to pour us more tea. "Someday you'll feel it. Don't worry."

"You know this writing stuff is your fault, don't you?"

Grandma sighs, and all of a sudden she looks sad. "I've been accused of worse."

"I'll dedicate my first book to you."

"That would be lovely, Morgan le Fay. Just lovely."

We sip our tea and talk about anything and nothing. Then a thought strikes me. "Why did you come back?"

Grandma's surprised. "Come back from where?"

"All your tours. You had the opportunity to get out of Central Nowhere, so why didn't you stay gone?"

"Why would I want to?"

I give her my best annoyed face. "You know it's my greatest desire to get out of here."

Grandma sighs. "My family was here. Your dad, your aunt Marilyn, and your Grandpa Marvin. I needed to come home because I *wanted* to see them." She's got on her remembering face. "I was so lonely out there, and I missed them so much! And we didn't have cell phones then." Now she's smiling. "Nobody could text. What a shame!"

"Oh, stop it." I, unlike others, am not attached to my cell phone 24/7. But I don't leave it in my room, either.

She's giving me a serious look again. "You want to get out of here that much?"

"More than that much." I sigh. "There's nothing here for me."

"You might change your mind, you know. Home isn't such a bad place to be." When she sits back in her chair she smiles like the Sphinx, like she knows way more than she lets on.

"We'll see." I try being Sphinx-like back to her, but I crack up. So does she.

A man falls in love through his eyes;
a woman, through her ears.

Hunan Pacific, Portland

I am going to kill Derek.

We're at my locker, and he gives me a quick kiss before he heads off to shop class. "Bye. I love you."

My wave is weak. "Back at you." I can't say it, because the guilt threatens to make me throw up every time I think about it.

Then weird old Mrs. Lewis, our biology teacher, shouts, "Break it up, you two!" We're not touching anymore, but she comes and yanks Derek away from me.

I try to be nice. "Mrs. Lewis, it's all right! It was just a quick kiss!"

Derek puts his arm around my shoulders. "And anyway, she's gonna be my wife pretty soon."

I shake his arm off my shoulders and give him an elbow in his stomach.

Mrs. Lewis' eyebrows rise into her hairline. "Are you pregnant, Morgan?"

Holy God. I elbow him again. "No, I'm not pregnant."

Derek jumps in. "It won't be for a while, but we're definitely getting married."

Mrs. Lewis backs off. "All right then." She skulks back into her room.

I whack Derek with my books. "Are you insane? Why did you *say* that?"

Derek laughs and massages his chest where I hit him. "I told you I was serious." And he waltzes off with a smile and a wave.

Now the teachers will talk, and people will check out my stomach.

At least it will balance out the lesbian rumors.

Those who laugh loud also cry hard.

Kowloon Panda, Charlotte

I'm trying to get into *Rabbit, Run* and failing miserably, when Martin plops on the couch next to me. "Guess what."

"What up, dawg?" I'm glad to close my book.

"I still say it's stupid." He tries to stick his finger in my ear.

I bend it back onto his hand. "What?"

"Gangsta talk. Ouch."

"How may I help you, Martin?"

"I've heard two rumors about you."

"Which ones?"

He leans in close, even though there's nobody else home. "I heard you're pregnant and I heard you're a lesbian."

"You didn't hear I was getting married?"

"Do you want to?" His eyes are wide.

"Not this decade."

He stretches out his legs to reach the coffee table. "So you're pregnant."

"No."

"You're a lesbian."

"No." I bonk him on the head with my book.

"I figured I would know that."

"You think I'd tell you?"

"Yes."

He's right. I would. "Would you feel different about me if I was?"

He tries to dope-slap me. "If you were, I was gonna tell you about a lesbian who works down at the Tool Shed."

I catch his arm and twist it. "Who's this?"

"Her name's Evelyn. Her partner is Patricia." He rubs his arm and gives me a frown.

"They live over on Tenth Street?"

"Right." He tries to pinch me.

I grab his fingers and squeeze them. "No one was ever sure about them."

"Ouch! She told us. It ain't no thing at the Tool Shed."

"I can't believe it ain't no thing."

"It's not." Martin got up. "Seeya." And he leaves.

> Judge people by what they think.
> That is what they are.
>
> Sea Pearl, Toronto

It's after work on a Saturday night, and I'm walking over to Gas & Ass to see who's out and about. Martin's leaning on the building, trying to look smooth and failing miserably.

"Shouldn't you be home?"

He checks his watch. "I still have twenty minutes on my curfew." He cocks his thumb at his buddy Joseph. "Joseph's mom is coming."

"To the Gas & Ass? Isn't that sort of embarrassing?"

He shrugs. "Where else are we going to be? Later, sister." They walk off to talk to some other freshmen, but Martin turns back around. "By the way, did you know you have grease on your boob?"

I swipe at my chest, trying to see where it is, and then he shouts "April Fool's!"

I give him my best scowl. "Butthead!" He just smirks at me.

When I go in, I see this crowd of girls huddled up by the bathrooms, and Ingrid and Jessica are tucked in the center. I get closer, and Ellen McMurphy turns and looks at me. Then she leans back into the group and hisses, "She's coming!" I brace myself. I've been waiting for something like this, but I keep walking to the bathroom. I think about closing my eyes but decide I'd rather see my doom.

I'm almost to the bathroom door when I realize nothing's happened. Ellen's still looking at where I've been. I turn back to see what she sees, and it's Tessa. The group advances on her as one big body of arms and legs, all of them staring at her like she's a monster or a murderer. And Tessa keeps walking. Right toward them.

I am not that brave. In a thousand years.

They're chanting. It's very quiet at first—"dyke, dyke, dyke"—but it gets louder as she gets closer. Then they're shouting their lungs out—"DYKE DYKE DYKE DYKE DYKE!" Jessica's shouting along, and her face gets purple with the effort. To her credit, Ingrid isn't saying anything. She knows she's in the wrong place at the wrong time. But she doesn't walk away, either.

Tessa tries to stare them down as she walks. My heart is leaping out of my chest, but I stay sucked up against the wall. "DYKE DYKE DYKE DYKE DYKE!" echoes in everyone's ears, like thunder from the ugliest cloud you've ever seen. Tessa lowers her head and keeps moving, shoving by me and disappearing through the bathroom door.

"Break it up, goddammit! Go somewhere else if you're going to act like that!" Mr. Martinez, the owner, almost leaps over the counter, where he'd been carding two sophomore guys who wanted to buy cigarettes. "What in the holy hell are you doing? Next time you pull this kind of stunt, you are *out*! I know all your names!"

He runs back to the counter and grabs a pad of paper and a pen. Nobody's really scared of him—he yells at groups of kids if they're loitering (I love the word *loitering*), but he also knows we keep Gas & Ass going. This time, though, he looks serious. He keeps scribbling.

The group drifts apart. Jessica and Ingrid come out of the center of the circle and they see me staring, trying to shoot them where they stand with the anger in my eyes. Ingrid, at least, has the courtesy to look away.

I don't know what else to do but storm out of G&A and walk home. At least it's warmer than it was in January. I'm walking so fast I get home at the same time Joseph's mom drops Martin off.

> Judge people by how they stand there and
> do nothing when bad shit happens.

Over and over and over again, on at least ten sheets of notebook paper while I'm sitting in my room, wondering why I didn't follow her into the bathroom.

You are kind-hearted, hospitable,
cheerful, and well-liked.

Yum Yum Bling Bling, Milan

It's Sunday night, and I'm trying to glean Great American Novel ideas from *Fight Club* but I'm not getting very far. The phone rings.

"So why didn't you stop them?"

"Stop who?" It takes me a second.

"That damn freaking crowd of people yelling at me."

"What could I have done?"

"You could've told them to get lost. You could've told them to fuck off. You could've done anything but stand there!" She hangs up.

She's right.

Tonight it's my job to feed Evan and Martin, so I go to Grocery Land to get a frozen pizza for supper. The freezer door hangs open as I study the boxes. I don't know what they want—probably three-meat pizza. No veggies for us, because we're carnivores to the core.

Then Rob gooses me.

I screech and whirl around, then smack him with the

eight-pack of toilet paper I have in my hand. We need some of that, too.

"Holy *shit*, keep your hands off my ass!"

Rob's laughing so hard he's bent over.

My heart is pounding. "That wasn't nice!"

"I'm sorry." He's still trying to quit laughing.

I whack him again with the TP. "What the hell do you want?"

"To say hello, and that we need to do something again. Soon."

"Name the time and place."

Rob looks at me. "What about Derek?" He has a great way of ruining the moment, but that was the next thought in my head, too.

"Are you two still chatting it up at the G&A?"

He's flustered. "That was weeks ago. January or something."

"Yeah, well ... don't talk to him, okay? This is weird enough." I know I sound crabby, but all of a sudden I'm spooked. I know it's not right, what we're doing, and I know I should quit, but I don't want to. And I do want to, all at the same time.

Rob touches my arm. "Are you getting cold feet?"

I pull away and don't answer for a second. "Maybe. No. Yes."

"Which is it?" The fences go up.

"I'll work it out and let you know."

Not what he wanted to hear. "When you're ready, if

you're ready … let me know." He turns away and heads back down the aisle.

In that instant, I decide.

"All right, then, when are we leaving?" When he turns back around, I give him a bright smile to make up for my hesitance.

"I thought you had to make up your mind." His fences are still visible, but he comes back toward me.

"I did." I reach to grab his hand and squeeze it. "Now, if you were in my shoes, would you serve Evan and Martin more or less meat?"

Rob shakes his head and *regards* me for a moment. It's such a loaded word, and such a conscious action. I can't say I like to be *regarded* because I never know what the regarder is thinking about me, but I like to *regard*, so I do the same to him. It's so silent you'd think the whole store was listening to us. Maybe they are.

Then he reaches around me. "Do they need more or less protein? Do they want more or less grease?" He pulls out a three-meat pizza. "Will they care?"

I take the pizza from his hand. With a quick glance around, Rob picks up my hand and kisses it. From Derek, that gesture would be dorky as hell, but Rob pulls it off. I don't even giggle, though I think about it.

"Here's to North Platte. Gotta go." He gives me a grin and heads down the aisle.

Boss Man Steve comes by while I'm standing in line to check out.

"Well, hello, Morgan. How are you?" He does his best to look charming, but I'm not buying it.

"Hi, Steve."

"Not working today?"

"No, sir." I'm sure my smile is polite, but I turn my back on him.

"When do you work next?" He's still not going away. In fact, he's breathing on my neck.

I move so far into the checkout line I bump into Mr. Reynolds' cart, which then bumps into him, which then gets me a big frown from Mr. Reynolds. I give him an "I'm sorry" look and turn back around to Steve. "I don't know, sir. You made the schedule." I give him the sweetest smile I can, and he glares. But he finally goes away.

I go home and put the pizza in. Evan and Martin love it. Good choice, Rob.

I'm not a nice person. I don't help Tessa. I two-time Derek. I smart off to my boss.

I must take after my father.

Plan ahead.

Firecracker Duck, Santa Fe

Derek comes in near the end of my shift.

"Hey, good-lookin'!" He hollers it from the door when he comes in. Only about twenty people turn their head to see who said it, and who he said it to.

"Keep your voice down, huh?" I snarl, hoping it gives him a clue to my mood.

He's walking toward me. "Will you come hang with me tonight? Just for a little bit?"

"I have to read for school. Sorry."

"So how will I get into your pants?" Thank God he's close and quiet by the time he says that.

"Shut up."

"A guy's gotta try."

I flick him with my cleaning rag. "Go do something useful."

He strides toward the meat department and comes back with steak and potatoes about five minutes later.

I scan everything. "Maybe I'll have to come over for supper, if this is it."

He gets close. "If you did, then we could have some nookie later."

"You have a one-track mind." I bag his stuff and hand it to him. "Let's worry about nookie some other day." He waves on his way out the door.

I stock candy and stare out the window for a while. Nothing's very green yet, but you can feel the spring wanting to push through the leftover brown of winter. Then I feel a slam on my conveyor belt.

It's a box of Banquet frozen chicken. Then I see who put it on the belt.

I can't say a word. I scan the chicken and put it in a bag. She hands me money. I hand her change.

Tessa's voice can barely contain the venom. "You could've helped me." Big and proud, she gives me the finger over her shoulder as she stomps out the door.

*The mysterious side of your nature
makes you most alluring.*

Hunan Empire, Pittsburgh

I see the red truck out on the hill again. It's there when I show up, but not when I leave. And after I take Grandma's car back and walk to Food Fabulousness, I realize why it looks familiar.

I am more than a little pissed. It's *my* hill.

The store is hopping, no pun intended, since it's almost Easter. Everyone's buying ham and butter and potatoes and Marshmallow Peeps and whatever else goes into a fancy Easter dinner. I'm scanning the eightieth ham of the day when Rob slides up behind me.

"When are you on break?"

"After this customer." He heads to the back room, and I maintain my air of professionalism until the customer with the sixteen boxes of Peeps—and one potato—is gone. Then I page Carrie, this middle-aged mom with six kids, to come take over for me, and I scram to find Rob.

He's sitting at the break table right next to the time clock, whistling and drinking a Dew. "So wh—"

"Who the hell do you think you are, invading my space

on the hill?" My hands are on my hips and my feet are planted.

"Invading your space on the hill?" He doesn't know what I mean, so I make it clear.

"Out on the side of the valley—six miles west, then three south? I saw your truck today. That's my spot, not yours!"

"You go out there?"

"Yes." I pause. "When I need some quiet time."

"It's you! You're the yeller!" Realization breaks across his face like a wave. "What does it mean when you say *I AM A SECRET SEX FIEND*, pray tell?"

I close my eyes and hope the floor opens up and sucks me in.

No luck.

"How many interpretations of that statement could there be?" When I open my eyes, Rob's the one with the red face. For a change. "So how many times have you heard me?"

"Just once—the day you said 'fuck' ninety-nine times. I counted."

I sit down at the table, facing him. "What do you do out there? Obviously you know what I do."

"Watch the hawks, study the fields. Walk. What else is there?" He smiles. "Unless a person felt like shouting their frustrations to the heavens."

The sky always hears me, and the hills don't mind.

"Well, we're going to have to make a schedule. I don't want you out there when I'm there. It's my private spot."

My stomach feels funny, thinking about giving up my sanctuary.

"Then it's yours." Rob gets up and throws his Dew bottle in the recycling bin. "There are lots of hills out there, and lots of places to walk. If you ever want company, let me know." He strolls back out to the store, and I sit there, completely dumbfounded.

I always have to fight for what I want.

When his shift is over, I'm still up front with the zillions of people buying ham. He brings a bag of frozen peas through my line.

"Yum. Eighty-nine cents." I hold out my hand for the cash.

He gives me a buck. "Supper is cheap at my house." He leans close while I'm putting his peas in a bag. "Sometime will you show me why you're a secret sex fiend?"

I can't even look at him. He whistles his way out the door.

Thoughts are things, too.

Dragon River, Denver

My world is shredded. Grandma had a stroke.

Dad was at her house, fixing something outside. It's a rare thing for him to be there but he'll go if something's broken, and when he came in for some water, Grandma told him she'd been seeing things, all sorts of people and animals wandering in and out of her house. She'd been sitting in her chair all morning, waiting for them to go away. Dad didn't know what to do, so he took her to the hospital and some test found a blockage in one of the veins in her head. The hallucinations were caused by a lack of blood to her brain. Dad said it was a good thing he'd gone over in the morning. Otherwise, who knows?

I come home from school and find a note on the table: "Grandma in hospital. Evan with us. Come when you can. Anne." I have to ride my bike—which I never use— because I can't run there and I can't walk fast enough, so I ride like a banshee. For once, I'm glad this town is small.

I park my bike by a bench outside the hospital door, then proceed to kick the bench about nine zillion times, because I'm scared to death and trying not to cry and have no idea what to do besides kick the bench. Then I hurt my toe, so I sit down and sob for about three seconds, because if I let myself cry, I'll never stop. Ever. A nurse comes outside and asks if I need help, and I can see by the look on her face that she's been watching me for a while. I tell her no and she goes away. I make myself sit there for another two minutes.

When I get to Grandma's room, she's calm, but there's a shaved patch on her head where they've injected dye into her brain. She looks tough and mean with the bald spot, but she still has her Grandma smile.

"Holy shit, are you okay?" I run over and fling myself on the bed, hugging her tight. I don't even think about whether I could hurt her.

Anne frowns. "Mouth, Morgan."

Grandma strokes my hair. "Morgan le Fay, I am all right. I have to stay here and rest, and have some more pictures taken of my head, but the doctor says I get to keep my brain."

"I need your brain—and the rest of you!"

"I know you do, honey. I need you, too."

I look around the room. Anne's in a chair, close to the door, and Dad's standing behind her. Both of them are giving me a look but I don't care. All I want is a well Grandma.

Evan runs in. "Hey, come see what I found!" He jumps up on the bed with us. Good thing hospital beds are big ones.

I make room for him. "What'd you find, dude?"

"A room full of bicycles! You gotta see this!"

Grandma looks glad to see Evan, too. It's obvious she doesn't like this kind of spotlight. I give Grandma another hug, this time up where her arms are. "I'll be right back, okay?" I don't let go for a long time. If I do, she might slip away.

"Go check it out and give us a report." She smiles, but she looks tired. Evan and I head out, and Dad and Anne give us the eye again. Maybe they'll go home and I can hang with Grandma by myself. That would help. We could be just us, laughing and goofing off and making fun of hospital food. Something normal.

I don't want to admit she's old or that she could die. I refuse that idea.

Evan's room of bicycles turns out to be the physical therapy room, so I ask the therapists if he can ride one and they let him. He laughs and pedals while I watch. When we get back to her room, Grandma's asleep and Dad and Anne have gone home. Evidently they've decided Evan can walk home with me. I let him ride my bike and I walk behind, my face dripping with tears. He rides a block ahead, then doubles back. "Let's go, Morgan. Woo hoo!" He hollers while he rides, and I trail behind, walking slow. My whole body hurts.

She cannot die.

I will not let her.

Let there be magic in your smile
and firmness in your handshake.

Green Palace, Albuquerque

Grandma's out of the hospital, finally, three days later. I go
to bed at nine the night she comes home because I haven't
been able to sleep since she's been in there. Then it's three
a.m. and a boulder hits my window.

I bolt straight up in bed. Then I hear it again, more
gently this time—BONK on my window.

I look out my window and I see a big broad shadow,
so I open up. "Derek, what the *hell* are you doing?"

"Come out here."

"I was freaking *asleep*! What the hell do you want?"

"Just come out here." I see a flash of white teeth in the
dark. His smile always gets me.

So I go. It's cold, maybe forty, and I have on a T-shirt
and sweats. I do remember slippers.

Derek takes his coat off and wraps me in it. "Why
didn't you grab a jacket?"

I pull it close. "I'm not intending to be out here long."

"Why not?"

"Because I was *asleep*, dammit. What do you want?"

"You've hidden away since your grandma's been sick, and I've missed you." He gathers me in his arms and I let myself sink into them. Guilt pangs rip my stomach in half.

He gives me a tight squeeze. "I'm not kidding about marriage."

"Oh my lord, just shut up about that right now. I'm not in the mood." I pull out of his arms and stand back.

"I'm serious. I love you beyond words. I want to be with you forever." His arms hang in the air until he realizes it and puts them down.

"It's not something I can tell you right now." I can't make a decent argument, because it's three a.m., but I try. "I can't promise you anything—I'm seventeen. Get it? Too young to decide anything but what to wear to school." I stomp my slipper.

Derek comes to me and tries to gather me up, but I stay put. He tries one more time but stops when he sees I'm not budging.

"Look, I'm sorry. But you're amazing, beautiful, wonderful, and every other adjective in the book." Every bone in his body is sincere. "I want you with me. Forever."

I relent. A tiny bit. "I'm honored. Truly. I'd love to be able to promise you something like this, but I can't. I just can't. I don't know enough about the future."

"We could *make* the future—together."

I'm pissed. "Have you not been listening? I'm not ready to do that!"

He backs away. "I'm sorry." He looks a little shocked,

and a little sad. "Can I at least hold you? I've missed you so much." I don't move because I'm pissed. He motions me into his arms. "I won't talk about marriage again. I promise. Now will you come over here? I need to go to sleep, too, and you need to get back inside before anyone realizes you're gone. We'll save the staying out late for prom night, okay?"

Prom. Who cares about prom?

I look up. The stars are gorgeous at three a.m. Then I move back into the circle of his arms and we stand there, warm and together. For now. "I can't promise you anything." I say it to his chest, but I know he heard me. He sighs.

Finally, without a word, he lets me go, and I watch him melt into the shadows. When his car pulls away—he's parked half a block down—I sneak back inside. At least the floor doesn't creak.

Avoid marriage proposals from anyone under thirty.

I write it with the squeeze-it honey bear on six slices of bread. It takes two lines of text on each slice. Then I eat them all.

*You have a reputation for being
reliable and trustworthy.*

Real Chinese Yum Indonesian Cuisine, Singapore

The next morning I'm staring in the fridge and Martin strolls by, looking like a cat that caught a bird. He doesn't do smug often, but he does it well.

"So, Ms. Outside-at-three-a.m., how often do you do that?"

"Shut up!" I try to shove him in the fridge but he wriggles away. "Dad and Anne don't need to hear that."

"They're outside doing yard work."

"How'd you know I was out there?"

He rolls his eyes. "I heard you go. How else?"

"I was quiet."

"Except for the door slam when you went out." He smiles again, like the canary is trapped behind his lips.

"No way."

"I got up and looked, and there you were with Derek."

"I really let the door slam?"

"Yeah."

"At least it was just you that heard me."

Canary smile again. "Not quite."

"*What?*"

"Anne got up, too."

"She *did*?" My life flashes in front of my eyes.

He's pleased with himself. "She saw me and asked what was going on. I said you went outside to pick up a garbage can that was blowing down the street, and she didn't notice there wasn't any wind. Then she went back to bed."

All I can do is look at him.

He holds out his hand, palm up. "I know."

"Jeez!"

"I know." The hand doesn't move. "Pay me."

"Pay you what?"

"Money. Duh. For saving your ass."

"Get out of here."

He puts his hand down. "You really should pay me."

"I really should kick your ass."

Martin shrugs and strolls back to his room.

The continued nonchalance bothers me.

I head to the laundry room for a laundry marker. Andi McGinnis, in my study hall, has a jacket just like mine, and we always seem to wear them on the same day— lame—so I want mine ID'd. I'm digging through a box of stuff when I hear Anne clear her throat.

"What was the pressing need in the yard so early this morning?"

I look up and try for innocence. "Pardon me?" Manners seem important here.

Here's the Look of Doom. "I asked you what was so exciting in the yard."

"Um … well … "

"Derek came to visit, didn't he?"

I drop my eyes.

Her arms are crossed tight. "How did he let you know he was here?"

It probably isn't a good time to lie. "He threw a rock at my window."

"And you went outside, even though you knew we'd be angry with you?"

"Yes."

An even bigger frown. "Why?"

"Anne, he wants to marry me, and I didn't want him to wake up Dad. I wanted him to shut up, and I didn't know what to do, and I don't want to marry him!" I don't mean to say all that, but it bursts out.

She's surprised. "He wants to marry you?"

"Yeah."

"Do you want to marry him?"

"I don't think so."

I clutch my jacket like it's a life raft while Anne studies me. "Are you going to go outside again, if he throws rocks at your window?"

"We'll have all our fights in the daytime from now on."

"Will you run away and marry him?" There's a smile in her eyes that isn't on her lips.

"Holy smokes, no way!"

One more Look of Doom. "I won't tell your dad. But *do not* do it again."

"I won't!"

"The laundry marker's on that shelf." She points.

"Uh … thanks."

"No problem." She leaves.

Once I've marked my jacket, I go find Martin. I try to shove him under his bed, but he escapes again.

"You butthead! You *knew* she caught me!"

"And?" He smiles again.

I try to put him in a headlock, but he squirms out right away. "You're a buttwipe!"

"I knew she wouldn't get you in trouble." He smooths his hair where I've messed it up.

"How could you know that?"

"And she won't tell Dad, either. I trust her on that."

I grab for him one more time, but he darts away. "How do you know?"

"Because she didn't tell Dad it was me who broke the window." The kitchen window ended up with a big hole in it about a week ago. "I busted it with a stick I was twirling. She told him a rock flew up from the mower."

"You were twirling a stick?"

He blushes. "Shut up! I won't warn you next time."

"There won't *be* a next time."

He adopts a fatherly tone. "See that you learn from your mistakes."

"She's nicer than we think, isn't she?"

He strolls back to his bed and sits down to play his guitar. "Must be."

"You were twirling a stick?"

No reply, so I leave. He's as weird as Evan.

The phone rings.

"I saw you in the yard with Derek." This time I know it's Tessa.

"Are you spying on me?"

"I was up anyway."

"Well, keep your nose out of my business."

I hear a sigh. "Trust me, I wish I could."

"You're fully capable of leaving me alone."

She hangs up, and I slam the receiver down so hard I crack it.

Have serious fun!

Golden Garden, Chicago

By mid-April in Central Nowhere, it's finally nice enough outside to re-start the field party tradition. Derek wants to go to the first one, and I agree because I'm still chicken to break up with him. I choose to be the designated driver, because if alcoholism is genetic, I'm screwed.

We get there early, and a bunch of cars, headlights on, are arranged in a circle to make a party spot. Mostly it's his class, not mine. The Loser Girls Who Torment People aren't there, either, which is fine with me. Derek is his social-butterfly self and I'm nerdy old me.

He pays for cups, but I leave mine behind. I hate beer, and not just because of my dad. It stinks. Derek's friend Scott does this great thing where he cups his hand around the air and pretends to drink from his empty hand. He calls it "making the sign," and people don't notice that he's not holding a real cup.

So I make the sign and watch Elisa, this chick in my class. She's plastered off her ass, so she decides she'll be a smoker for the evening. She wanders in and out of groups of people, laughing louder than everyone else and blowing smoke in people's faces. When she's out of cigarettes, she goes off and pukes in the corn rows. A pack of smokes in less than two hours, I'm guessing. Grotesque. When she gets back from puking, she's more sober and she's stopped shouting "Oh, God! I'm so drunk!"—which is a blessing for everyone.

I see Derek in the crowd, but he disappears again before I can grab him. I'm stuck listening to his buddy Randy tell bad jokes.

"Why did God create blondes?"

"Why?"

He lunges for me. "Sheep can't bring beer."

I dodge. "You're so funny."

"Why did God create brunettes?" He grabs for me again.

I back up about eight feet. "Why?"

"Neither could the blondes."

"You are awful."

I turn to go, hands over my butt to keep Randy from pinching it, and Tessa's standing right behind me. She smiles in that wolfish way. "Just the girl I was looking for." Her hair is tipped in pink tonight. I can see by the glaze in her eyes that she's not sober, either. I'd seen her, of course, but I'd managed to stay out of her way.

"Hi." I try to move around her.

She grabs my hand and yanks. "Come over here."

"Where?"

"Over here. To talk. We haven't talked forever."

Precisely my plan.

She's strong, and she drags me outside the circle of headlights. I desperately try to find Derek as she pulls me along, but he's nowhere to be seen. When Tessa lets go of my hand, we're standing behind a car on the farthest side of the circle. No lights, no people.

I rub my fingers where she's squished them. "What do you want?"

"This." She grabs my face and kisses me.

I stand there. Something flickers, but I stay still.

She tries to get her tongue in my mouth, jabbing and prodding and mashing her face on mine. Finally she stops and steps back. "You liked it before!" She hollers it loud enough for the whole world to hear.

I'm as brave as possible. "I like kissing. Not you."

"That's not true!"

My gut is churning. "Yes it is. I don't want to be your girlfriend."

"You're a tease." She strokes her crotch and thrusts it toward me. "You just want to torture me."

"No, I don't … I just like to kiss."

"You're a fucking liar. You would've fucked me in your back yard if I'd asked you. I could tell!" She's breathing hard.

I turn around and start to walk.

"Morgan!"

I don't know where I'm going, but by some miracle the first person I run into when I come back into the brightness is Derek. I fall into his arms, and he steadies me.

"Morgan?"

"Take me home."

"What's wrong?"

"Nothing. Just take me home. Please."

"Are you drunk? I thought you were the DD tonight!" He tilts my chin up so he can look at me. I try to stare back. He must see something in my face, because takes my hand and leads me to his car.

If there was ever a cliché, it's "my lip quivered." But that's what it did.

I say nothing on the drive home. Derek walks me to the door and gives me a very sweet hug and kiss. "Can't you please tell me what's wrong? I want you to be okay. I love you."

My lip quivers again, very visibly this time. "No, I can't. I love you, too."

He gives me another hug and drives away. I can see the questions in his eyes from my front step. But I just can't tell him.

Maybe she had enough Wild Turkey. Maybe she won't remember.

Would I have fucked her?

Would I?

No day but today!

Lucky Pavilion, Montreal

On the hill, I shout and shout and shout but no words come out. It's one long yell.

When I get back in Grandma's car, I find a pad of Post-Its she keeps in the glove box.

> Beware of hallucinations when your brain
> gets clogged with field dust.

> Do not enjoy uninvited kisses.

> To avoid unwanted confrontations, stay home.

I rip them into tiny, tiny pieces and get back out of the car, then I sit as still as I can on the hillside and open my hand. The words blow away.

Your love life will be happy and harmonious.

Golden Sky, Fort Worth

Rob's waiting around back for me in his two-tone red truck, and he's pissed.

"Why did I have to park back here?" He hollers it as I walk toward the truck. "Why couldn't I just wait at Gas & Ass?"

I get in and slam the door, which I really don't mean to do, but if he's going to start it I might as well continue it. "Everyone at G&A knows Derek is my boyfriend, and I don't want people gossiping about us."

"You think people aren't talking?"

"Please tell me they're not." I'm not in the mood to hear it.

"Even Boss Man Steve asked me the other day if we were dating. I told him it was none of his business."

"That's just because he's a sleazy bastard and he wants to ask me out himself."

"That may be, but if he's hearing it, who's saying it to him?"

The silence is loud, because I don't answer him.

"Morgan?"

I cross my arms. "What?"

"I don't know how you feel about this two-timing thing, but it's getting old. Really old. It's not my business, because you're the one who needs to decide what you want, but it's not fair to Derek *or* me to keep it up." He's tapping his hand on the side of the car, out the open window, not looking at me.

I sigh. "What exactly are we doing?"

"I don't know! Are we having fun as friends? Are you feeling more than that? I know I am. But I promise I will leave you alone, and ask Steve not to schedule us together, if you don't make a decision." Tap tap tap. He's serious.

I try to turn on the sweetness. "Oh come on ... we've got to at least work together. We have too much fun."

He turns to me. "No. I can't take it. I think you're smart and funny, and I love being with you and you're really cute, but I'm done with the secrets."

I'm really cute?

I notice his nostrils all of a sudden because they flare when he's angry, so I close my eyes and try not to laugh. This is a serious moment. "You're right. Of course you are. I'm horrible, and it's not fair to either of you."

"So who do you want?"

I look at Rob. "Who do you think?"

He's calmed down a little. "You need to say it and mean it, Word Girl. Use your words." He puts his hand on my shoulder, which gives me shivers.

He's staring, so I do my very best to stare back. All I want to do is look away, but he won't let me.

"Do you need a moment to decide?" His eyes are still locked on mine.

"I've decided."

"Who is it, then?"

I'm going to throw up, but I say it anyway. "You."

He lets out an enormous sigh. "I'm so glad."

"I have a lot to do, like break up with Derek."

"I can wait."

"It's more than just Derek, actually."

"Excuse me?" The hand disappears from my shoulder.

"There's a girl in my class . . . and, um . . . she likes me. She just kissed me at a party." It's most of the truth, anyway. And it's a relief to say it out loud.

"Oh." It's obvious he doesn't like this news.

"It's weird."

His eyes get narrow. "Do you like her back?"

"I wouldn't be hot for you if I liked her."

He's moved way back in the corner of his seat. "Are you sure?"

Am I? I look at his face. I'm sure.

"As sure as I can be about anything right now." I give him a tug back into the middle of the seat. "All right?"

"All right." Rob grabs the hand I tug him with and kisses it. Open-mouthed. On my palm.

I try not to melt away while I talk. "You need to know what's on my plate, and you've got to help me by being patient."

He's nibbling my fingers. "I can do that. If it means we get to be together."

"Thank you." My voice is a little faint, and it's a good thing I'm sitting down.

"For you, no problem. And hey?"

He looks up, leans over, and kisses me. Really kisses me. A tongue and stars and flip-floppy-stomach kiss. Finally. I don't kiss him as hard as I want to because I don't want to scare him, but holy scamoly, he is delectable.

When he pulls away, he smiles. "Just that."

I have to catch my breath. "Okay. Could you turn on the air?"

Rob laughs. "Shall we go to North Platte?"

He starts the car, and that's what we do.

Keep your feet on the ground even
when it crumbles beneath you.

Golden Dragon, Macon

Saturday shifts at Food Casa are torturously boring in
spring—it's gorgeous outside. And no Rob, either—he's
with his dad, doing whatever farmers do. It's so nice out
I ride my bike around after work. Then I decide to go to
Grandma's. I look in the kitchen window when I park my
bike in the driveway and there's water's running in the
sink, but I see no Grandma doing dishes. I look in the
garage and her car's in there, so I go inside. The house is
silent except for the gushing faucet.

Boring is over.

I shut the water off. "Grandma? Hey, it's me, Morgan."

No answer.

"Grandma? Are you here?"

I hear a little bump sound, but that's it. No Grandma
in the kitchen or living room. No Grandma in the music
room. No Grandma in the basement, which is good,
because the stairs are steep and we keep bugging her not
to go down there. No Grandma in her bedroom. I look on
the far side of the bed, in her closet, everywhere. I look in

the guest bedroom: no Grandma. Then I notice the bathroom door is shut.

"Grandma?" I knock as loud as I can. "Grandma, are you in there?"

"Wh … wh … who is it?" Her voice is muffled.

"It's Morgan! I'm coming in!" I pray she's not on the can.

I open the door slowly, in case she's in the way or on the floor. I don't see her when I first look in, and that scares me more.

"Grandma?"

"I … uh … in here, honey."

The shower curtain's drawn. When I pull back the curtain I see her, crouched down with her arms over her head. Since it's Saturday she's wearing what she calls "work clothes," but it's nothing like regular-people work clothes because she never wears jeans or T-shirts. Her button-up shirt and slacks are a wrinkled mess, and her hair is a wreck.

"What's wrong? What happened? Are you okay?" I'm so scared I'm shaking. But someone has to hold it together.

Her face is white and flat when she turns it up to me, and she looks like she's just waking up. "Morgan? Honey? When did you get here?"

"A few minutes ago. Why are you in the bathtub?"

I help her stand up, and her knees crack. It takes a while to fully unbend her. When I help her step over the side of the tub and come out of the bathroom, we go slow as turtles because Grandma's legs are shaky. She looks around like she's not sure where she is. I get her sitting down in her chair, and I kneel in front of her so she'll be sure to see me.

"Tell me why you were in the bathroom. Please? It's okay. Nothing will hurt you."

She smiles her beautiful Grandma smile, the peaceful one that makes me feel all right. "Oh, dolly, you'll think I'm silly."

"I won't. I promise."

"Well … there were kids in here. More than one. They were messing with my stuff, and jumping out from behind furniture and yelling 'Boo!' and scaring me. One of them started throwing dishes out of the cupboard, and that's when I went to hide in the bathroom."

"What time was that, do you know?"

"I think it was around noon."

I look at the clock. It's four thirty. I look around to see if anything is messed up. No broken dishes on the floor, no newspapers scattered around, just general piles of things to do.

"I'll let Dad know some kids were here. Is there anything I can do to help you right now?"

She frowns. "Don't tell your father! I don't want him thinking I'm some crazy old woman."

I pat her hand. "He wants you to be all right, and you can't be scared in your own house. Now please tell me what I can do."

The confused look is back. "What are you doing here, Morgan?"

"I was just coming to chat. To get some good Grandma advice."

"About what?" Her eyes are a bit brighter.

"Oh, you know ... boys. And this girl kissed me."

"That's so nice. She must like you."

"Grandma!" That's not the answer I expect.

"It's just a kiss, honey." Her voice starts to fade. Then her eyes fly open.

"Morgan!" It's like she's seeing me for the first time this afternoon. "Did I ever tell you?"

"Tell me what?"

"How sorry I am ... so sorry."

"Grandma, there's nothing to be sorry for. Not a single thing."

She sighs. "Oh, my love, I wish you knew ... oh my ... " I can see she's hurting. "Could you help me into the bedroom? I'm exhausted, and very sore." I don't think she has any idea how long she'd been in the tub. "What time is it?"

"Four thirty."

She stands up, and I hold her arm as she walks—so slowly—into her bedroom. She takes off her shoes and lies down on her pink bedspread, and I cover her up with a blanket from the closet. I gave her that spread when I turned twelve and she turned sixty-three.

"Good night, sweetheart. I'm glad you found me." She's already closed her eyes.

I gulp the tears away. "Good night. I'll see you soon. I love you." I lean over and give her a kiss on her cheek, which is the softest skin I've touched in my life. By the time I stand up, she's already asleep. She looks peaceful now.

I, on the other hand, am *scared. Frightened. Terrified.*

Before I let myself out, I make sure the other doors and windows are locked, in case they really weren't hallucinations. I lock the door behind me when I go.

My pedals say "sick, sick, sick, sick, sick" as they push me home.

Dad does *not* take the news about Grandma very well. He's reading the paper at the kitchen table. Anne is nowhere to be found, nor are Martin and Evan.

"She was where?"

"Hiding in the bathtub. The dry bathtub."

"For how long?"

"I'm not sure ... maybe four hours or so."

"Holy Jesus! What the hell is going on?" He storms over to the phone. "Goddamn woman." I don't think he's too far into the beer fridge, but it's hard to tell the difference between drunk and angry with him.

"Let it go, Dad. I can take care of her."

He slams the phone down, and the crack I made in it gets longer. "No you can't. You're seventeen. I'm taking care of it."

"Yeah, looks like you're handling it real well. Good job."

I see the anger come over his face as he starts to spit out words. "You. Ungrateful."

"Rude bitch, right? I remember."

"Shut your mouth, Morgan, before I shut it for you."

I have no idea if this is an idle threat. He's never hit me before, but there's always a first time.

"Just be nice to her, will you? She's your mother."

He starts to huff. "Remember what I told you about the spatula? That's not all she did. One time she locked me outside in January. Once she wrenched my arm so hard I couldn't play baseball for a week!"

All the blood drains out of my body. He's drunker than I thought. All bets are off. "Shut up. She's really sick." He can't disrespect her like that.

Dad's face is the color of a fire truck, and he's breathing like he's run ten miles. "You think that's all? Your aunt Marilyn got the hairbrush, but I got spatulas, rolling pins, and belts." He can see that I don't believe him. "Don't think so? Ask her someday about the Saturday she chased me with a baseball bat and I had to hide in the neighbor's garage until she calmed down. Try explaining that to your friends, why you're hiding when they're looking for you, and why your mom's off the deep end!"

My mind goes numb.

He's still puffing. "See this scar?" He points to the back of his hand, to the crisscross of tissue raised on his skin. "Compare it, in your mind, to the metal spoon rest on her stove. What do you see?"

He's right. It's the same pattern.

His eyes are nailing me to the wall. "Think how hot it was to make this kind of scar."

"Shut up, asshole! You're lying!"

"This is too big for you, Morgan. You can't understand,

and she's got you fooled anyway. She lies to everyone, and she's lied to you for fourteen years."

He turns away to accost the phone, and I can't think of what to do, so I run to my room and write *People lie* and *I hate my family* and *Trust no one* at least ten times each on three sheets of paper. Then I take the pages into the kitchen and find the matches. I light them on fire, one by one, and throw them in the sink after they burn down to my fingertips. Dad is nowhere to be seen.

Then the smoke detector goes off and he storms up from the basement. "What the hell is that smell?" He sees me in the kitchen. "What the hell are you doing?"

I light a pile of paper napkins, throw them at him, and slam out the door. The smoke detector cries for me.

I walk and walk and walk, going nowhere. Finally I go to Grandma's and find her secret car key in the garage, tucked under the spare bottle of motor oil. Thank God her bedroom window is far away from the garage or I'd wake her up with the door. I think about going in to check on her, but I have no idea who I'd see: the grandma who loves me, the woman who has hallucinations, or the crazy lady who burned my dad. So I swipe her car and drive out to my hill.

By spring it starts to take a while for the sun to go down in Central Nowhere, especially since we live two hours from the line that starts a new time zone. When there are no clouds, like tonight, the sun creates soft bands of watercolor paint that spread across the entire sky, like a vista-sized parfait of air and fading light. Usually it's the most beautiful thing in the universe, but not tonight. I want blackness.

My dad is a fucker. But if my grandma abused my dad, it explains a lot about him.

So why is she so nice to me?

I read somewhere there are five stages of grief: denial, anger, bargaining, depression, and acceptance. Sometime during the night I go through each one, though I usually skip acceptance and go back to anger. When the moon comes up I scream at it: no words, just screams. When the coyotes call I scream at them, too. Finally I can form some words, so I start with *I HATE BRADLEY MARVIN CALLAHAN* about fifteen times. Then I holler *I HATE ELSIE YVONNE CALLAHAN* about five times, but then I feel so disloyal I lie on the ground and weep until I can't catch my breath. When I'm silent again, I hear the coyotes talking to each other. I try to follow what they're saying, in case they've got some good advice, but their yips end up blending into one long howl.

I don't go home until the parfait starts to recreate itself in the east and I have no voice left. Grandma's car goes back in her garage, and I walk home. When I get there, it's light. Martin's eating cereal at the kitchen table, and he stares when I go by. On my bed, there's a note: "Grounded until further notice."

Of course.

Be proactive, not reactive.

Lucky Seafood King, Tucson

The grounding lasted for three days. Now Dad won't look at me, and that's fine, because I won't look at him. Last night at supper he told us Grandma hasn't had any hallucinations since the bathtub incident. That's good. But I'm not talking to her right now, either.

Since everything else in my life is disintegrating, I decide it's time to find Derek and have the talk. I bike over to his house and look in the window. He's sleeping on the couch, but I walk in anyway.

When I ease myself next to him, I admire the view for just a moment. He looks like Adonis or Hercules sleeping off a long night of chasing goddesses. For about six seconds I reconsider, then I remember I'm tired. Tired of bad sex, trivial conversations, and everything that's easy and boring.

I shake his shoulder, gently as I can. "Derek."

"Hunh? Wha…Morgan?" He can't figure out what happened. I'd be the same, if I fell asleep by myself and suddenly Derek—or Rob—was there. He reaches up and pulls me to him in one of his big hugs. When I put my head on his chest, I start to cry. That wakes him up.

"What? What's wrong?"

All I can do is wail.

"Did someone die? Did your grandma die?" Derek sits up but keeps me close.

"N-n-no." It's hard to talk.

"Then what the hell is wrong? Honey, calm down."

"I can't!" Off I go again.

He holds me for a bit and doesn't talk. That's good. Finally I can look at him because the waterworks are slower. "I have to tell you something."

"It can't be this bad." He can tell I'm serious.

I sniffle. "Yeah it can be."

"What are you talking about?"

"We need to break up."

Derek sits back a little and looks at me. "You woke me up to break up with me?"

I feel the waterworks starting up again.

"Then why are you crying?" He pulls me close again.

"Because I don't know if I want to break up with you! But I have to!" That sends me off into even more tears. My chest hurts almost as bad as it did the night I spent on the hill and I'd guess some of these tears are leftovers from that occasion, but he doesn't have to know that. After a thousand sobs I take a deep breath and wipe my nose with my sleeve. "Okay."

"Okay what?"

I take another deep breath and push myself away from

him. "I need to break up with you because I can't marry you, and I can't stay in this town. Please don't ask me if I love you, because I do. But we have to be done."

Derek stares. "You're serious."

I try to stare back, even though tears are still trickling down my face. "I'm serious."

He doesn't say anything. But then his face changes. "What about prom, Morgan? It's two weeks away. Who am I gonna take to prom?"

Leave it to Mr. Dipshit.

I jump to my feet. "Stupid goddamn *prom*? Two years together and that's all you can say?" I want to slap him, but I don't. "I'm outta here."

I crash out of the house and glare through the window as I wrench myself onto my bike. Derek is sitting absolutely still, staring at the door. I don't think he knows what hit him.

I have lots and lots of energy to pedal with. What an asshole. I cruise around town for a little bit, burn some anger off, think about going to see Grandma, decide against it, and head to the Grocery Yurt. The red truck is in the lot.

When I walk out of Aisle 12 to head to the break room, I'm slammed into the green bean display. Cans fly everywhere, including onto my foot, which hurts almost as much as my shoulder does from getting smacked.

"Oh, wow, excuse me, I'm ... hey! It's you!" Rob picks me out of the mess.

"Dammit!" I rub my shoulder. "Slow down the next time, would you? That hurt!"

Rob rubs my shoulder, too. "Sorry. What a way to start your night, huh?"

"I'm not working. I came to see you. Guess what?"

"You wrote the Great American Novel?"

"I broke up with Derek."

"You did?" He grins, then wipes it off his face. "Well, that's too bad."

"Not really."

"Oh?"

"Yeah." I grin back, to let him know it's all right to resume his own. He goes back to the produce aisle, and I trail behind. The mound of lettuce heads he's been creating threatens to tumble down because he's not paying attention to what he's doing. We're too busy laughing and talking.

Isn't there an appropriate mourning period when you break up with someone? I bet it's longer than twenty minutes, but I really don't care.

What is popular is not always right,
and what is right is not always popular.

Teahouse of the Gods, St. Paul

In between classes today, Derek comes to my locker. He looks very, very worried. I managed to avoid him all day yesterday, and he called a bunch of times last night, but I told Evan to tell him I wasn't home.

"I've been looking for you!"

I shut my locker and turn to face him. "I'm right here."

"Why haven't you answered my phone calls?"

"I don't know what else to say."

"I didn't dream what happened?"

"No."

He's pissed. "You won't change your mind?"

"No."

"Fine. You are the worst fuck I've ever had!" He stomps off.

"I'm the only fuck you've ever had!" I shout it at his retreating back. His shoulders push back, and he straightens up while he looks around to see who heard me. Lord knows we couldn't embarrass Sir Manly. Amazingly, no teacher sticks a head out of a door to crab at us for our profanity.

I hope his little tiny dick explodes without its Friday and Saturday night workouts.

I slam my locker, trying to remember where the hell I'm going, and Martin is behind the door.

"What was that all about?" He's obviously surprised his sister was just yelling obscenities in the hallway.

"We broke up the other day, and Derek was just making sure I meant it."

"Did you?"

My brain finally clicks, so I start to walk toward study hall. "Yup."

"That's big." He's amazed.

"Yup."

Martin walks off to wherever he's going, still looking at me like I've just sprouted another head. Maybe I have.

In study hall, Tessa tries to catch my eye but I make sure to memorize every line of linoleum underneath my desk.

After school I'm walking to work, and Ingrid's car, the Green Limousine, pulls up next to me. Like the day hasn't been weird enough.

"Hey, Morgan! Want a ride?" Jessica's hanging out the passenger window and waving. Since the Gas & Ass incident I've steered clear of them, too. Really clear. Ingrid and I still talk a little at lunch, but I have nothing to say to Jessica. So I'm surprised to hear the shout, to say the least.

"Where are you two headed?" I climb into the back seat, even though I'm not sure I should.

Ingrid answers. "Wal-Mart, for prom stuff. Want to come?" It sounds like going to Cheap Plastic Crap Mart is low on Ingrid's list of things to do.

"I've got to go to work. Can you drop me?"

"Sure. How've you been? We haven't seen you much." She's cautious but friendly.

"Things are a bit … strange right now. I broke up with Derek."

Jessica turns around and stares. "We heard. Prom is two weeks away! What are you going to do?" She makes it sound like I cut my arm off and was proposing to do a cartwheel with one hand. I couldn't do a cartwheel with three hands.

"I'll go with someone else, or I'll stay home."

"It's *prom*! Don't you understand that?" Jessica's eyes beg me to grasp this horrid situation I've put myself in.

"It's just another night."

Ingrid snorts, and I wonder who she's going with.

Jessica's appalled. "It's the biggest night of your life!"

Thank God we're at Food Fiesta by then. It's that time of the month again, and blowing my stack would be as easy as saying goodbye. "Thanks for the ride." I hop out.

"It was nice to see you." Ingrid's eyes are sincere and she keeps darting them at Jessica, sort of to say, "I'm sorry for this nut job."

"Good luck, Morgan." Jessica still looks horrified.

I wander inside, and Mrs. Anderson is trying to untangle a

cart from the metal rack. I help her with a smile and a friendly hello, just like we're supposed to. She's so surprised she smiles back.

Boss Man Steve is standing by the milk cooler as I'm heading to the back room.

"Hello there, Morgan. You're looking happy today."

I curb the monster that leaps into my throat, threatening to roar. "Hello, sir. I'm having a nice day because I don't have to go to prom." That part is true. It's honestly not my thing—it requires a trip to Girl World, after all, and I might not have enough makeup ability to pull it off again. Derek and I went last year, and I felt stupid all night long. Nobody expects me to go without him, anyway.

He smiles in a way that says, "In my brain you have no clothes on," then he clears his throat. "You're not going to prom? Well... that's too bad." I see the lightbulb go off over his head. "Um... would you like to..." He's almost salivating.

"I've got to punch in, sir." I scramble around the corner like a mob is chasing me.

Rob's sitting at the break-room table waiting to punch in, and I give him a kiss on the cheek and a punch on the arm at the same time. My internal monster's gone elsewhere.

"What's with you?"

I grab my time card. "Life's insane. Did you know that?"

"I did."

And we go to work, because there's nothing else to say.

Use the tools you are given.

Red Moon Garden, Los Angeles

The word *love* is a tool. It's a crowbar. You can get yourself into all sorts of places—someone's pants, someone's heart, someone's life. And it's a hammer, too. Lots of people swing it with no idea of who they'll hit. In fact, you can pound the shit out of people with that word: Dad on us, or Grandma on Dad. But Derek probably has hammer marks from me. And Tessa might, too.

So maybe I should stay away from Rob. What if I put a dent in his head, or sink the claw into his cheek, and all he's trying to do is *love* me back? What if that's all I know how to do? What in the hell do I know about a concept like *love*?

I used to wrap myself in Grandma's *love* like it was a soft, cozy quilt.

Love is one of the worst words on this planet, but I still like the word *planet*.

> Procrastination is the belief that the
> greatest labor-saving device today is tomorrow.
>
> Imperial Delight, Baltimore

Today in study hall Tessa throws me a note, and I can't
ignore it because it's folded up tight and hits me in the
side of the head.

I rub my temple and get up to throw it away. But her
face is too sad and I can't take it. So I bring the note back
to my desk and unfold it, which takes a while. She'd bent
it up good.

"Can we please talk? I'm sorry if I scared you."

She's not making undying love declarations, so I make the
universal symbol for "call me" and go back to my algebra.

I'm not in the house five minutes when the phone rings.
I think for a second before I answer it. But what good does
it do to ignore the situation? We've been doing that since
last summer.

"How are you?" She's hesitant.

"Uh ... fine."

"Wanna drive around?"

I pause. "Okay."

Tessa zooms up as I walk outside. She drives a total

'70s car, a Trans Am, I think. It has some sort of bird wings painted on its hood and a T-top, too, which is opened up because it's sunny and beautiful. It looks kind of cool even though it's old and beat to shit. I barely get in before she's backed out of the driveway. She looks as nervous as I feel.

"Where'd you get this car?" It's an easy way to break the ice.

"It was my dad's, when he met my mom. It used to be really cool."

The upholstery's ripped, the carpet's matted, the dash is cracked, and everything in it has faded from red to candy pink. It smells like dust.

"It gets me around, and I love the T-top. Except when it rains. Then it leaks." She sighs.

"It suits you. Not the beat-up parts, I mean. It's attitudinal." I notice the empty Wild Turkey bottle on the floor in the back seat.

She keeps her eyes on the road. "I think so."

We drive with no plan. Up one street and down another. She must not be worried about gas prices.

She clears her throat. "Are you going to prom?"

"No. I broke up with Derek."

"I heard that. Brave move."

"Are you going?"

She puffs out her chest. "I'm wearing a tux."

"Clever."

"Can you imagine me in a dress?"

The picture in my head is awkward. "Well, no."

Big pause. She clears her throat again. "So ... let's talk."

"What do we need to say?" I make sure my voice doesn't squeak.

"I remember what happened in the field. I wasn't that drunk."

"Um … okay."

"I've had a crush on you since eighth grade. You need to know that."

Nobody says anything for a few streets. I suck it up and get brave when we drive by the Grocery Garage and I see the two-tone truck.

"It's really nice of you, but I can't love you that way. You know that, don't you?" I check out the houses going by instead of her face. "You're a great kisser, and I really do love kissing, dumb as that sounds. But I don't want a girl-friend."

Tessa sighs. "I figured as much. But the chance was there, so I took it." She stares at the road. "I'm glad you said it."

"Why?" I risk it and look at her. She doesn't seem mad.

"You're being honest with me, which is what I was doing with you in your back yard. I'd been sitting on that secret for such a long damn time. It sucks to love someone who doesn't love you back."

"I know."

She doesn't believe me. "How could you know?"

"You should see my family."

Tessa rolls her eyes. "Oh, please. This is hormone love. Sexual love. Like you love Derek, or you used to."

"Okay, so maybe I don't know." I feel my whole body

206

get hot. "Forgive me for not knowing how to handle this." I move next to the door. Sexual love. But duh.

"So let me make sure: this is it for you and girls? You're swearing off forever?"

Now the hotness has moved to my face. "Well…"

Tessa laughs, long and hard. At least she doesn't say, "Ha! I knew it!"

Nobody talks for a minute. Then something occurs to me. "It's got to suck, being a lesbian around here."

Her eyes stay straight ahead. "Why do you say that?"

"It's probably not something you can tell a lot of people."

"In this town, all people know is that lesbians are ugly butches and gay men are drag queens." Then Tessa pauses. "Actually, you'd be surprised who *is* like me in this place." Now there's a smirk on her face.

"Evelyn and Patricia at the Tool Shed?"

"Yeah, but there's more. Think study hall."

"Study hall?"

"Who always throws me notes?"

"Amber Sibley."

"Right." Her grin is slightly wicked.

I'm so dumb. "Which explains why she can't take her eyes off you." Then my brain clicks again. "What about Caitlin Hanson?"

Her grin broadens. "Still working on her." Then she's serious again. "But shut up about it. Would *you* want to be outed in this town?"

"No."

"My parents don't even know."

"Why not?"

"You'd be able to hear the shouting in Omaha." It's obvious she's sad about that fact.

"What about Amanda and all the rumors? I saw her one night in your yard, and she slapped me on the street one day after school."

"Really?" Tessa's laughing. "I didn't know she slapped you."

"Is it true that her mom caught you guys in bed?"

She nods.

"Why didn't Amanda's mom tell your folks?"

"Who wants to admit their daughter's a lesbian?" Her smile is sly. "But that's okay—we had sleepovers at my house instead."

I laugh. "You're out of control."

"What else is new?" Her hair has rainbow spikes today.

"How do you do that to your hair?"

"Bleach and Kool-Aid."

We don't talk for a while, which is fine. Now the silence isn't full of emotion. But then I start thinking about the other craziness in my life, and I see a woman with white hair, all crouched up and scared in her bathtub. "I wish it was this easy with my grandma."

Tessa startles. "Your grandma's a lesbian?"

"She's a child abuser."

"Nobody's grandma is a child abuser."

"If I believe my dad, she is."

Her face clouds up. "How can anyone believe what a dad says? Ask her instead."

"That's what I mean—I wish talking to her was as easy as talking to you about that damn kiss."

"You think this is easy?" She cranks the wheel to swerve into a light pole, but relents when she sees my face. "I bare my soul to you, and you reject me!"

I can't tell if she's serious or not, so I study the houses again. "I know. And I'm sorry. But it wouldn't work."

"Oh, give it up. I know it wouldn't work—you're 99 percent straight, and I knew that last summer. But you can't stop a girl from trying, can you? Especially with the benefit of liquid courage?" She pokes me in the leg. "Or is it closer to 90 percent? What about 80 percent?"

I ignore her last comment. "Maybe I'll get drunk and talk to Grandma. That should go over like a pregnant pole vaulter." A Grandma expression.

Now Tessa swerves by accident because she's laughing so hard.

Then we're back at Tessa's house. I walk around her garage and head to my own house. "Thanks for the ride."

After a pause, she calls after me. "Are you still going to be my friend?"

"Yeah." I turn around and give her the peace sign.

Once I'm in my yard, I notice a Post-It note on the air conditioner. It's water-spotted and beat up after the winter snow. You can't read it at all. I leave it alone.

> A woman who has only her beauty
> is a business heading for bankruptcy.
>
> Jade Lotus Blossom, Little Rock

Prom is next week, and I'm checking out the dresses in the teenage-girl-angst-look-at-me magazines we have at Sack O' Eats, since no one's come through my checkstand in an hour. Some of the dresses are described as "stunning tulle creations," which means the skirts of those dresses are Scarlett O'Hara all over again. I thought those kind of dresses were out, but it shows what I know. The slinky ones are "smooth and sophisticated matte jersey," and one dress was made of "sassy and demanding organza." How does anyone know if a dress is sassy or demanding?

> Do not listen to your dress if it talks to you.

I have a prom dress from last year that I didn't wear, a deep midnight blue one, and I adore it. Derek fell in love with it, too, and we waited forever for it because it was on back order. Then when it came, I didn't look like the woman in the magazine—I bumped and bulged in places the model didn't. Derek was pissed, and I was so pissed at him that I didn't wear it. I wore some ugly mint green thing I picked up for really cheap. That was one of our first big fights. I should have known.

I can't tell if this prom stuff is bumming me out or making me mad. Maybe I should just wear the damn blue dress and go by myself.

Right.

I'm stuffing the magazine back in its rack and I hear "don't put it away!" from down the aisle. Rob's booking toward me, and he grabs the magazine before I get it replaced.

I grab it back. "What's your deal?"

"I want to see which dresses you like." He leafs through the pages.

"Why?"

"We're going to prom, aren't we?"

"We are?"

I've never seen anyone's face actually fall, but his does. "We aren't?"

My surprise is obvious. "I didn't know you wanted to."

"Now that you're not with Derek, what's there to stop us?"

"Well … nothing."

"Exactly!" Rob looks pleased as he studies the dresses.

I stuff the magazine back in its rack. "I'm not sure about this."

"What's not to be sure about?"

"I'm not sure I want to go to prom at all, or maybe I want to go by myself."

His eyes narrow, but his voice is calm. "I thought you

wanted to be with me." He turns on his heel and strides down the aisle.

"That's not what I meant!"

He whirls around to face me. "How many more ways are there to interpret that comment?"

"Come back here. I can't shout all the way across the store."

He takes a few steps toward me, so I try to flirt a little. "I won't bite you."

"I'm not convinced." But he takes a few more steps.

"I can't choose for myself about prom?"

"I've waited all school year for you to be single, and now you don't want to go with me?"

"I hadn't thought about it like that." I really hadn't.

"You're too damn selfish to think about it like that." He turns around again and gets a little farther away.

"Don't go. Please?"

He turns back slowly. His mouth is set.

I try flirting again. "Can we talk about this without being twenty feet apart? Please come up here."

He walks back to me. "You've made your position pretty clear."

"If I take you to prom, people would think I was two-timing Derek."

"You were."

Goddammit.

I close my eyes. "You're not even in high school any-more. Why does this matter?"

His footsteps go away. I open my eyes again and he's down at the other end of the aisle, glaring at me.

I try one more time. "Do you want to get a tux to match my dress or just a black one? My dress is midnight blue."

He leaves the aisle without another word, and I am an instant puddle of misery.

Crazy Gus chooses that moment to step into my checkout line. He's clean, which is the first surprise, and the second surprise is his wide assortment of food: an apple, frozen brussels sprouts, tomato juice, and popcorn.

He's radiant. "Hello, young lady. How are you?"

I try to get my act together. "I'm all right, sir. How are you?"

"I'm clean, literally, and also sober. It's a great day."

I give him a faint smile as I bag up his food. "That's $12.73."

He hands me a twenty. "Keep the change."

"Sir, I can't do that." I hand him his $7.27.

"Yes you can. Things change. People change. Here's my change." He throws it onto the belt and waltzes out the door. He waves at the people coming in. They stare.

That was random.

Something else thunks onto my conveyor belt. It's a bottle of Mountain Dew, with Rob attached to it. He doesn't look at me.

"$1.29."

He digs out two dollars and hands them over. I put the change in his hand while I grab him with the other one, so he's trapped. "Look, I'm sorry."

He pulls his hand away so he can open the Mountain Dew, then he frowns at it and scowls at the candy.

"You need to order your tux soon, or they won't have any. Prom is next week."

"What makes you think you can just apologize and it's over?" It's a growl.

"I don't know. Hope, I guess."

And then the worst thing happens: the tears start to roll. The cash register keys blur in and out as I try to make them stop, but it's no use.

Rob doesn't notice until I blow my nose, because he's chugging his Dew. Then he can't stop staring.

"It's okay! Please don't do that! I'll get a black one. I'll drive to Kearney, even, to find one." He's desperate to make me stop, and he hands me Kleenex after Kleenex until he empties the box next to the register.

I sponge off my eyes. "Are we done with the prom discussion?" I blow my nose again.

"I think so."

I can barely hear myself. "Then can you come over here and hold me?" The tears start again.

He's still on the customer side of the conveyor belt, so he braces himself and vaults over. "What's wrong with you?"

The tears take a pause. "You just leaped over the counter."

"What the hell is wrong with you?" He enfolds me.

I can't say anything for a while, and he holds me while I shake. If Boss Man Steve could see us we'd be fired, but he's not here and no customers are interested in being inside on a Sunday afternoon in May.

"What's the trouble?" He rubs my back until I can answer him.

"My grandma."

"What's wrong with her? Is she sick again?"

"I don't know. I haven't talked to her forever."

He steps back to look at me. "You can't go two days without talking to her!"

"My dad told me all the things she did to him." I point to my hand. "He has a scar that matches a spoon rest in her kitchen."

"That can't be."

"The scar is proof. And it would explain why he's so mean to us—wouldn't it?"

"I suppose it could." He squeezes me again. "You've stopped shaking." I don't say anything. "The only way you'll find out the answer is to talk to your grandma. And even then, this stuff would have happened a long, long time ago. Neither of them remembers everything." He grabs a paper towel from the roll he finds next to the paper bags. "Your mascara is down on your chin." With all the gentleness in the world, he wipes my face. I can't believe I let him do it.

"I'd rather chop my arm off with the meat saw than talk to her about this stuff."

"Too messy. And how would you hug me?" He gives me a swipe on the nose with the paper towel and one more squeeze. "Are you better now?" His smile is so tender I could melt right there.

"Yeah. Mostly."

"So I can get back to work?"

"Go manage something, Mr. Assistant." I try to sound bossy, but I'm too tired. "I have candy to face, and I bet you have freezer backstock melting on the floor somewhere. Like by the freezer."

"Maybe someone's come by and stolen a pizza or two." As he walks away I watch his cute, sweet ass.

A million things are racing through my brain. Grandma. Dad. Rob. Derek. Prom. Lingerie—all I own is underwear, so I need to get some lingerie, pronto. Toenail polish. Cute sandals. Cute handbag. Grandma. Dad. Rob. Derek. Tessa.

There's a drawer in the checkstand, so I put Crazy Gus' change in there, in an envelope I find, and label it with his real name—Arnold Gustafson. I also find a pad of gift certificates for a turkey drawing we have at Christmas, and three times on the back of each certificate I write:

People are more complicated than the formula to figure the Gross Domestic Product of an industrial nation.

There are sixteen certificates, so by the time I'm done, my shift is over and my hand is one massive cramp.

An ass may go traveling,
but he will not become a horse.

Good China Sky, Oakland

Tessa and I are outside. She's kind of my new Girl To Sit By At Lunch, for better or worse. We sit on a bench in the sun and talk about skipping for the rest of the day. Then we watch people going to their cars to make out. The PDA ban gets tough about noon.

I stretch. "Got your tux for prom yet? You'd better, considering it's in three days."

"Are you going?" She tries to snuggle close and I give her a push.

"With Rob, a guy from my store."

"Does Derek know?"

"No, and don't tell him."

"Why would I want to ruin the surprise?" She wiggles her eyebrows up and down. "Is this Rob guy gonna beat him up?" She tries to sneak close again.

I stand up and move to the opposite end of the bench. "I don't know. He'll probably ignore Derek."

"Well, that's no fun either."

I sigh. "Can we pick another definition of fun?"

She jumps to her feet and assumes a macho man pose. "I put the 'FU' in 'fun,' so I'm sure I can figure something out." Then she sits down to slide close to me again. "Let's just hold hands. Derek will be so glad you're bringing a guy to prom instead of me, he'll forget about everything else."

I try politeness. "This is more fun than I want today."

She puts her arm around my shoulders. "No problem."

I give her a giant shove, and she about falls off the bench, she's laughing so hard.

"Not funny, Tessa."

"Yes funny, Morgan. You really have to lighten up." She punches me in the shoulder. "And guess what?"

"I have no idea."

"I found a place with a chef program! Can you believe it?" She looks pleased with herself. "And guess what else? They don't care that I'm still in high school, so if I want, I can take classes this summer. I'll be ahead of the game."

I give her a smile. "See? Easier than you thought."

"Way easier. Thanks to you." With lightning speed, she reaches over and gives me the shortest hug on record. I hug her back, just a tiny bit.

Then Jessica is standing in front of the bench. "You let her hug you!"

"And?" Tessa rises to stand between Jessica and me.

Jessica looks around Tessa to me again. "She's a lesbian! You can't let her touch you." Jessica half-whispers, half-hisses this information, and points to Tessa like Tessa can't hear her. Like an avenging angel, Jessica's feet are spread and planted, ready to defend anything that threatens her.

I stick out my tongue. Very middle school, but I'm sick to death of her stupidity. "Hugging a friend is not a big deal."

Jessica shudders. "What if she gets the wrong idea?" Another whispered hiss.

I shrug. "We've already talked it out."

Jessica backs up six inches at least, to be safely out of range in case Tessa takes a swing. "That's just gross!"

I stand up, too. "Tessa's not contagious, and how would you know if it's gross or not?"

Jessica sniffs. "I just know."

Now Tessa's laughing. "I had no idea you'd been with a girl."

"I'm still a virgin!" Jessica shouts it in Tessa's face, loud enough that people coming back from their PDA snacks turn and stare.

Ingrid has wandered up behind Jessica and starts to laugh, too. "Glad the world knows your sexual status."

Jessica whirls around to face her. "Tessa gave Morgan a hug, and Morgan hugged her back!"

Ingrid's still laughing. "You're so small-minded."

She sputters. "How dare you talk to me that way?"

"Give it up. Tessa's not threatening your virginity." Ingrid gives Tessa a smile. "Or are you?" Tessa is in hysterics, and I just wait to see what happens. Nobody talks to Jessica like that.

Jessica stares, like Ingrid's told her she's lost the Miss America pageant. When she speaks again, she's so frosty you can see her breath, even in the spring air.

"For your information, Ingrid—and yours, too, Morgan—I don't have to put up with anything I don't approve of. And I have every right to say so and do so. This is the U.S. of A., and we have freedom here."

Ingrid sighs. "Obviously you've been listening in government. But it still doesn't mean you get to say stupid shit all the time."

That, apparently, is enough for Jessica. She gives us a look that says we're scummier than the deadest leaves under a compost pile. "Lesbians are sick, gross, and morally wrong. I'm leaving." She huffs away while we watch her go.

Ingrid plops down at one end of the bench. Tessa picks the other. I sit in the middle.

Ingrid turns to me. "So what do you think, Morgan?"

"Dunno. Think she'll forget?" I give her a smile. "I'm never hanging around with her again."

"I'm joining you." Ingrid stretches out, catching rays on her legs. "She probably won't talk to us anymore anyway. She doesn't like to be called stupid, even indirectly."

"But she IS stupid." I close my eyes and feel the sun on my face. I have no desire to go back to class.

Ingrid presses her skin to see if she's getting any color. "Her parents are narrow-minded, too."

"Obviously." I sigh and turn to Tessa. "What do you think?"

She shakes her head. "Dumbest girl I ever met."

The three of us talk and laugh in the sun until it's time for algebra.

Don't force it; use the proper tool.

Emperor of the Sun, London

My dad is at the table when I come out for breakfast. Normally he's gone by the time I get to the cereal, because he's got a new job as a salesman. Paper products—how exciting.

He's sober in the morning, so it's the one time he's relatively nice.

Crunch, crunch. He doesn't say hello first.

"Hey, Dad."

"Hey, g'morning. Want some cereal?" He doesn't notice if I eat—ever. And he actually seems cheery. I don't know if it's because he's got a job, or because it's morning, or if another of his multiple personalities is talking.

I grab the cereal and find a bowl. "Yeah … um … can you tell me something?"

Crunch. "What do you need to know? I'm brilliant." He smiles.

"That's why I thought I'd ask." Flattery works every time with him.

"Shoot, then. I've gotta go in a minute."

I sit down at the table. "Tell me more about Grandma and you."

"What about us?" I practically see the wall slide into place.

"Do you remember what you told me about her? That she used to ... hurt you?"

Now the crunching is CRUNCH, CRUNCH. "Nothing to say. Case closed."

I decide to push, but with context. "I thought maybe you could help me. We've been studying child abuse in my psych class, and I'm wondering if you'd theorized about what happened. If you'd tell me, I could quote you in my paper. I won't use your name, of course."

He doesn't know I won't take psych until next year.

He snorts, like he does when he's getting ready for a lecture. "I do understand more now, yes."

I wait.

He clears his throat. "It turns out she had severe PMS—that's a real medical diagnosis, for your information—and she was also under a lot of stress, traveling all the time. So every month, if she was home, things got scary when the hormones kicked in."

He's got to be kidding. I fumble. "That ... um ... must've sucked."

If it's really a diagnosis, it might explain why I want to kill people around that time.

"Don't say 'sucked.' Aunt Marilyn was her favorite because she liked school and was polite, and I hated school and was too mouthy. Plus I did stupid stuff, like blowing up things with cherry bombs because I was pissed she was gone all the time. That made her even angrier."

This is news to me. "You were pissed she was gone?"

"Sure. Who wants their mom to be gone half the days of the month, every month, all year long?"

I didn't expect that answer in a million years. "I can see your point. What did you do to piss her off?"

"One time we blew up a trash can, and it went five feet in the air, which was cool as hell, but Mr. Lindberg didn't think so. One time I egged a car and took the paint off it. Once I sent Marilyn down the stairs on a sled, when she was little." He's trying not to smile but I can see he wants to. "So she took it out on me instead of everyone else."

Crunch, crunch.

I think about it for a second. Then I figure I might as well go for broke.

"Do you forgive her? That's another thing we gotta put in—whether or not we think it's okay to forgive abusers." No map for this territory, and I could be shelled by a hostile army any second.

Crunch. Pause. "I'm not sure. It's complicated."

"How so?"

"I know she's sorry, about a million things, and she tries to apologize sometimes, so I try to listen. But it's hard. Goddamn hard."

He stands up, strides over to the sink, and thunks his cereal bowl inside it. "Discussion closed. Hope your paper goes well." He hurries out like his ass is on fire and he has to find a river to sit in.

School is a total loss because prom's tomorrow and nobody's paying attention, including the teachers. I slip off to the library and type "severe PMS" into Google and I'm flooded with information. There are even court cases where women were given lesser sentences because their crimes were committed under the influence, so to speak.

She really was *crazy. Nuts. Barmy. Round the bend. Mad. Insane. Psychotic. Mentally ill.*

So what will I do to my children?

But I shut that thought down—not today. No time. Don't want to know.

At some point during the day, I wander by the gym to check the progress of the decorations. The junior class always decorates for prom, and I am grateful as hell I didn't sign up to help. Jessica, however, is in full glory in the gym, bossing everyone around and flirting with the guys building the props. Her sweetness oozes into the hall and threatens to wreck my shoes.

Speaking of that, I still don't have any shoes for prom. But I know someone who has an amazing shoe collection, from all her years on stage, and she has the same size feet I do—we are also shoe twins. So after school I walk to Grandma's.

Usually it takes me fifteen minutes to get from school to her house, but this time it's an hour because I walk around all the blocks three times before I get to hers. My stomach is in knots, but I have to know.

I see her in the kitchen and I knock on the window.

She jumps, but when she sees it's me she moves faster than I've seen her move in a long time. The door flies open.

"Morgan le Fay! How are you? Where have you been? It's been so long! How are you? How's school? Oh, Morgan, I've missed you! Hasn't Anne told you that I've called?" All of this is said in the midst of the biggest hug in the world and about ten kisses. It's all I can do not to cry. Anne told me that she called. I just didn't call back.

"Hi, I'm good, I'm fine, I'm ... sorry it's been so long. School. Work. You know, all that kind of stuff." I try to give her a smile, but I don't think it's convincing because she doesn't smile back.

"Come in, honey, and have some iced tea. Can you stay a while?"

"Not too long. And actually, I came to borrow some shoes. Prom is tomorrow, and I don't have any to go with my dress."

"Why don't you have prom shoes? Doesn't every girl plan for prom for six months in advance?"

"It's a long story."

"Then by all means, let's hit the shoe closet."

She gives me her Grandma smile, the one that says she loves me. I have to look away.

Back behind her music room is a walk-in closet full of shoes. When I was six she showed me her shoes for the first time, and I fell in love with a pair of red satin pumps that I wore around her house every time I came over. Nobody else's grandma had a shoe closet like hers, and I made sure to tell every girl I met about it. I'd even bring them over, and they'd ooh and aah and get jealous. Now Grandma and I both wear a size ten, and when my feet finally hit that size, I was thrilled to death. Granted, I have to dress up to borrow most of them, but they're available.

Just like the first time—when she takes me in, I gasp. The place is amazing. I haven't been in here in forever.

Grandma's regular shoes are on racks in the middle of the floor. She lets me borrow the ones she doesn't like, which are usually the most fashionable ones because she'll see a pair on eBay she thinks are great and she'll buy them because she wants to be young again, but when they come in the mail, she'll hate them. Some of the walls are full of performance organ shoes, which are like her red lace-up numbers—the heels are square and not very high. Some of the racks are full of shoes she wore when it was just Grandma and the piano in the middle of the stage, and those are the shoes I need today—high heels in endless colors. Some of them are old-school ugly because the styles are so stale, but some are retro cool.

I pick out three pairs—black patent, pink satin, and navy blue snake—and make for the chair in the corner of the closet.

"What color is your dress, honey? Why didn't you bring it with you?"

"Um … I didn't think about it. I only decided to come over after school." I try on the black pair. "When did you wear these?"

"Carnegie Hall, 1977. It was a full symphony, so we had to wear our penguin outfits." That's what she always calls the black skirts and white blouses she had to wear when she played in ensemble. The colored shoes are usually from solo events.

"Why would people in New York care about the Omaha Symphony?"

"Lots of reasons—there are some great soloists who live out here who even people in New York want to see."

I try on the pair made of navy snake. She went through a snake phase in the '80s. "How the hell did anybody find a blue snake?"

"They're dyed, sweetheart. I don't remember when I wore those." She frowns. "My memory isn't so good right now."

I keep my eyes on the shoes. "How are you feeling? I should've asked you when I got here."

"I'm ... all right. I haven't had any more hallucinations, or reasons to get in the bathtub, at least." She sits down in the chair next to mine. "I've missed you so much, Morgan. How have you been?"

"I'm ... good. I think. That girl I told you about?"

She looks confused. "You told me about a girl?"

"Yeah. She kissed me, remember?" She nods, the clouds finally clearing. "It was weird. And I broke up with Derek, so I'm going to prom with Rob, the guy I have a crush on from Food and Fun."

"You've had a busy love life!"

"Maybe a little too much so." Maybe a lot too much so.

"Does Derek know you're going to prom with Rob?"

"No."

"How was it to have a girl kiss you?" She's got a look in her eye. "Obviously you didn't melt."

"No … we're friends."

"That's good, honey. I'm proud you've worked it out."

I try on the pink satin pair. They're fantastic, strappy, open-toed sandals with at least three-inch heels.

"Where did these come from?" Even though the toes are pointy and the heels are thin, they're comfortable. It doesn't make sense. I prance across the room to look in a floor-level mirror, then prance back to my chair.

"They're from a private concert I played for President Ford in 1988."

"He wasn't president in 1988—was he?" I try to remember what we learned in government.

"No, but he was born in Nebraska, so he was here to dedicate his boyhood home as a historic place. I played a few songs."

"Can I borrow them?"

"What color is your dress?"

"Midnight blue."

She laughs. "I used to do that, too. Even when I was wearing the penguin outfit, sometimes I wore flashy shoes that didn't quite match. Peony pink will be beautiful with midnight blue."

I take them off and put on my scruffy Etnies. "Thanks for the loan."

"Any time, Morgan. For you, anything." She searches my face to see how I take that last comment, and I look at her chin, her shoulder, her feet, anywhere but her eyes. But I've got to know.

"Grandma…"

"Are you going to tell me why you've been gone for so long?"

"Maybe." I'm going to heave all over the shoes. "Dad told me something."

She sits back in her chair. "I can only imagine."

"So I need to know what's true and what's not."

"I'll do my best to tell you my side of it."

I can't look at her. "He said … you hurt him."

She doesn't say anything for at least a minute. Then she leans forward in her chair and reaches out to take my hands.

"Morgan, my lovely birthday gift and my shoe twin, he is right. I did hurt him. What exactly did he tell you?"

"He said you beat him, yelled at him, and locked him outside in the winter. You had psychotic PMS."

She sighs deeper than I've ever heard her sigh. "Every month I'd lose it, a thousand times worse than a woman with regular PMS, and I lost it at him more than anyone else in our family. Much more."

"Couldn't anybody help you?"

"Once the doctors figured it out—stupid men doctors—the medicine helped, but it was too late. Even with the medicine, things weren't perfect."

"There's medicine?" The stone in my chest gets a little smaller.

"I didn't get it in time. Your dad was in college, and the

damage was done." She takes a deep breath. "He has every right to be angry and bitter. I've always hoped he'd forgive me, but that doesn't seem like it's happened, has it?"

"He says he considers it sometimes."

"Well, that's something, I guess. If I could take it all back, I would. I'd give away my talent to get back those times. But I can't. So I try my best to make it up to him by loving you with all my strength." Tears are threatening to spill out of her eyes, though her voice is calm. "Is that why you haven't been here?"

"I ... didn't know if I should believe him. I didn't want to believe him."

"I'm sure you didn't." I see her breathe in again. "Is that all he told you?"

"There's more?"

"Well ... " The exhale is long. "There's one more thing."

My heart starts to flutter again. "Isn't this enough?"

"Oh, my dear one, I wish it was." Her eyes are full and sparkly.

"What else could there be?"

She closes her eyes. "You know how your mom died, right?"

"In a car accident. I was saved by my car seat."

"Do you know why the accident happened?"

"There was a reason?"

I can barely hear her. "When your mom ran a stop sign, her door was smashed by a driver going through the same intersection. That part everybody knew." Now the tears are coursing down her face. "But people didn't know she was mad at me, so she probably wasn't paying attention."

"Why would she be mad at you?"

"Because I...slapped you. And shook you."

I'm speechless.

"I was in menopause, so my moods were a constant mess, and you scratched a CD of the music I needed to practice, and..." She looks at me with the saddest face I've seen on a human being. "And I couldn't control myself. She snatched you away from me and was rushing home to tell your dad. And I had to tell him...after...the accident."

I can't breathe. The world is far, far away, down a long tunnel.

"Morgan? Honey?"

I have no way to move my muscles.

"Birthday twin?"

Then the anger roars into me, and I jump up and kick over the closest shoe racks. "You did fucking *what*? You *hit me*? You hit my father and then you hit *me*? What kind of a horrible person are you?"

"Honey, I know you can't understand..."

"No, I fucking can't! You're my only ally. My only support!" I crumble to the chair. "I can't...I can't...you hit me! And you killed my mom!"

She reaches for me and I shove her away and turn my body into the corner of the chair. I can't hear anything but my own wails.

I'm hoping I'll die. I'm hoping the shoes will fall and a

stiletto will pierce my heart, or the ceiling will cave in, or a nuclear missile will hit this house. Anything.

Anything to take away what she said.

After a long, long while, I uncurl myself and wipe my nose on my sleeve. But I don't leave the chair. I tuck myself up into a tiny ball again and don't move. I have no desire to see any human being ever again.

Why didn't somebody tell me?

After what seems like years, the shoe closet door opens and a head peeks around it.

It's my dad.

"Honey?"

I can barely see him because my eyes are so puffy. "What?"

"Can I take you home?"

"Is she out there?" I have no idea when she left, but she did.

"Yes."

"Do I have to talk to her?"

"No."

"Then you can take me home." I stand up, which is hard to do because I've been curled up in the chair for so long, and grab my peony pink shoes. When we pass her, standing in the kitchen, I can see she's been crying, too. But I don't look at her for more than a second.

In the car I want to throw up, but I breathe as deep as I can and the urge passes. When I roll the window down the air feels good on my face.

My dad's being very cautious as he drives, so I'm not convinced he hasn't been in the beer fridge already. He clears his throat. "It's probably good you know. It might help you understand some things."

"She hit you! She hit me! She stole my mother! What's there to understand?"

"She's also been trying to make it up to you since it happened."

"All of her kindness has just been canceled. Why the fuck should it matter now?" Then I realize I just said *fuck* to my dad, and I wait for the explosion.

"One giant act of badness doesn't cancel out all those years of goodness, does it?"

When he puts it that way, I can see his point. Sort of. Marginally. I cross my arms and stare out the window. "Doesn't mean it wasn't horrid. And it's not like you let her make it up to you. Why should I let her make it up to me?"

He ignores the last comment. "No, it doesn't. But she's regretted it since the day it all happened." He sniffs, and I notice he's crying, too. "She would do anything to make it better."

If my dad is crying, it must mean Armageddon is tomorrow. As does the lack of explosion about the F-bomb.

"Melinda was so wonderful." He looks both ways three times as we move through an intersection. "My reaction to the situation wasn't good, either. I mean, look at me—I'm an alcoholic now, and I barely drank when she was alive." His sigh is as deep as Grandma's was. "Grief is awful."

I don't know what to say.

"But that was a long time ago, and we should both do our best to forgive her. Especially you, Morgan. You are the light of her life. After the accident, she had a hysterectomy so the hormones would be permanently gone. And as you know, she is nothing but kind and generous to all of us even though I'm not so nice in return. But she adores you extra hard, so you'll know how sorry she is."

I think for a minute. "I can't believe I trusted her."

"You trusted her because children are resilient. You loved her before it happened, so you forgot and loved her after it happened." He turns onto our street, going way slower than the speed limit. "So now you know."

"Whether I want to or not."

"Maybe. But things might make more sense now."

I don't answer right away. "Maybe."

We're home, and my dad looks right at me. He never looks anyone in the face. "Please don't shut her out of your life. It would kill her."

"I'd think that would be okay with you."

He whacks the steering wheel. "This is not the time to be a bitch, Morgan!"

"Excuse me? Who are you to talk about being an asshole?"

He shoves the car door open and slams it once he's out. By the time I get inside, he's already downstairs in the beer fridge.

Anne's in the kitchen as I go by on the way to my room. "Honey? Are you okay?"

"Not really."

"Cut your dad some slack. Please? He's been figuring out how to tell you this stuff for a long time."

The tears threaten again. "Why did anyone have to tell me at all?"

"You deserve to know." She's as sad as everyone else. "You are so much like Melinda. That fire in you comes directly from her."

"I didn't know you knew her." Another secret.

"We knew each other in college. I always liked her, and your dad, too. When she died, your dad kept to himself for a long time. Then he reached out to people who knew Melinda, and that included me. And you know the rest of the story." Her smile is still sad. "I know he wishes he didn't drink."

I give her a hard look. "Hasn't he ever heard of treatment?"

"He tried once before, you know."

"He did?"

"When you were ten. Remember that month-long trip he went on? It wasn't for work."

I stare at her. "What is up with this family and its secrets? Isn't it more healthy to get it all out there?" My stomach threatens to erupt again.

Anne gives a small laugh. "How about if we treat this as a new leaf and turn it over?"

I can't laugh in return. "Works for me."

She goes back to cooking and I wobble to my room and crash on the bed. I don't hear her when she comes to tell me supper's ready. When I wake up again, it's seven thirty. In the morning.

A closed mouth catches no flies.

Yum Yum Blossom, Berkeley

Today I will forget everything I learned yesterday and be a normal seventeen-year-old. What the hell else is there to do? I'm too tired to cry.

I can't ignore the fact that my shaking hand just jabbed my eyeliner pencil into my eye. Ingrid called earlier and asked me to get ready at her house, but I didn't want to do one of those bullshit group things, nor did I want to go to the hair stylist with her. For what? I'm not about to pay a ton of cash to have someone poof it up when I can do that myself. My hair ends up more spiky than poofy, but that's fine. I think about finding the Kool-Aid and bleach so I can and tip it with blue, but I restrain myself.

I paint my toes a pretty metallic pink to match my shoes, and then I put on my corset-thing and my dress. Overall, not a bad effect. I pick up the beaded evening bag Anne loaned me and go out to the kitchen.

Evan's at the kitchen table, very calmly writing his numbers. When I come in, he stops. In fact, he drops his pencil. "Wow, Morgan. Are you going to get married?"

I hug him and give him back his pencil. "Close your mouth, dude. It'll be years before I get married, and you'll be invited if it happens. Okay?"

"Okay." And he goes back to his columns and figures. But his look of amazement makes my day.

Our house has the oldest burnt-orange shag carpet on the planet (there's that word again), and my heels keep getting stuck in it. Once I make it to the door, I shout that I'm going outside to wait for my prom date, if anyone wants to take pictures. I really don't expect a response, but I thought I'd offer.

About a second later, Anne follows me out.

"Is Dad coming out to meet my date?"

Anne squints in the sun. "He'll be up in a second." Must be peeing out all his afternoon beer. "What lovely shoes. Pink and blue is a good combination, I think."

"They're Grandma's."

"Very nice. Are you going to tell us who this mystery man is?"

"You'll find out for yourself in a minute."

"Will we like him?"

"I should hope so. He's perfectly respectable—no piercings, no colored hair."

Anne frowns. "You know that's not what I mean. Is he nice? Is his family nice?"

"He seems just fine to me."

Suddenly Rob is there, in the convertible. His tux is absolutely gorgeous. He is absolutely gorgeous. And the flowers in his hand are absolutely gorgeous. *Gorgeous* seems to be the only word I have left—my vocab has gone to prom ahead of me.

"Hey! You brought the fancy car!"

Rob's smiling like I've never seen him smile. "My dad was kind enough to let me take it." He stares at me. "Wow."

I'm so glad it's him in my driveway instead of Derek.

Rob sticks out his hand. "Hello, Mrs. Callahan. I'm Robert Jensen, but everyone calls me Rob."

Anne shakes his hand and smiles. "We're very happy to meet you. How do you two know each other? Morgan's been very quiet about her prom date."

"We work together at the store."

"How would you like to line up west of the house? The sun is best there." Anne leads us over to a spot next to a bush, and we both laugh into her camera. She clicks a few.

"Can I put your flowers on?" Rob hesitates when he holds them out, like I'm going to say no. Anne takes more shots of Rob pinning on the corsage. The flowers are pink, blue and white. I got him some, too—blue and white.

"How could you have known about the pink shoes? I just picked them out yesterday!"

Rob smiles. "I'm just that good."

"A couple more photos, kids, and you can go." Anne snaps a few more.

We're walking back over to the car as my dad slams his way out of the house. "So, this is the mystery date? Why didn't you ask my daughter to prom more than a week beforehand?" He sounds stern, and slightly drunk, of course.

"Yes, sir, hello, sir. My name is Rob Jensen. It's nice to meet you."

"Don't do anything stupid tonight."

"No, sir. We won't."

"Well, then ... have fun."

"We will, sir."

I give him a wave. "Bye, Dad. Don't wait up."

He frowns. "What time will you be home?"

"Remember? We decided I could be home by five."

He shakes his head. "I don't remember that."

Anne steps in. "See you by five, honey. Enjoy yourselves!"

Finally, finally, finally we get in the car. I sigh as we pull away. "I'm sorry about them."

"They seem perfectly all right, except that your dad is drunk and it's four in the afternoon."

"You have to come by before noon if you want him sober. It's Saturday."

"You don't have to worry about them for the next twelve hours." Rob reaches over and takes my hand. I've been waiting all day for him to do that.

We decide to go to the junior pre-prom-party-pin-up-pushover place, or whatever it's called. When we pull up, I check out whose cars are around, but I don't see anyone threatening.

"Rob, your car is the nicest one here."

He hops out and comes around to open my door. "It always is."

The party's crazy busy, so we slide right into the crowd

and head for the punch table. Ingrid's there with her date, Charlie Baxter. He's a senior.

"You look beautiful!" Ingrid hugs me and we try not to crush each other's corsages.

"You, too, Ing. Where's Jessica?"

"I don't know, but I don't think you should be here when she gets here."

"Why?"

"Well, Matthew dumped her the other day, so she found a prom date at the last minute."

This isn't gossip I know. "Why did he dump her?"

"I dunno—maybe he got tired of her stupid commentary, too. Crap-ola! There she is!" Ingrid's looking over my shoulder. Her eyes are round.

When I turn around, there's Jessica. And Derek, holding Jessica's arm.

I check them out for a second, then turn back around. I breathe in and breathe out.

Rob's across the room, but he sees the expression on my face and hurries back. "Are you okay?"

"I think so. My former boyfriend just walked in with my former friend." There's an ache in my chest I didn't expect.

"Should we leave?" He looks worried, like someone could get hurt. And someone might. I don't know.

I think for a second. Then, in my head, I hear a tiny voice say, "Fuck it," so I take Rob's hand. "Let's see what happens, shall we?"

He smiles back. "I can handle that."

As we mingle, I keep my eye out for Jessica and Derek, but they're always on the opposite side of the room. I'm not sure they've seen us, because the place is pretty packed. When Rob takes my elbow and steers me toward the door, I keep my head down, looking at my pink sparkly toes in their pink shoes. I won't have to see them if I focus on my feet.

"Morgan!"

Spotted. I look up from my hooker shoes. "Hey, Jessica." I give her the kindest look I can manage, which is pretty decent, actually. I have the man I want. All of a sudden, my chest feels better.

"Isn't that the dress you bought for last year?" Jessica smirks.

"It is, actually. You look great. I like your date." I have to throw that in.

Jessica looks pleased. "Isn't it nice? Matthew, that asshole, dumped me a week ago. Then I saw Derek at Wal-Mart two days later, and we decided to come together since both of us had our hearts broken."

I can't tell if she's serious or sarcastic. I squeeze my hands together, because they're itching to slap her. "We're off to find our spots at the banquet. See you later."

Throughout this exchange, Derek doesn't blink. He's standing behind Jessica and I think he expects us to come to blows. I smile at him, turn around and take Rob's hand, and walk out. Derek's eyeing Rob, and I can see the wheels turning in his head.

I swish my dress while we find the car. "Dude! Look at my feet! Aren't they sexy?"

"All of you is sexy. Trust me."

I add a little skip to my walk. "But don't you love my shoes? They're kind of hooker shoes."

Rob holds the door open for me so I can get in. He didn't do that at home, which is too bad. It would have impressed Dad and Anne. "I think 'hooker shoes' is an appropriate label. Did you get them at Frederick's of Hollywood?"

"Only drag queens shop there."

Rob walks around and gets in. "How do you know that?"

"Their shoe sizes go up to really huge."

"So where did they come from, if not Frederick's of Hollywood?"

"My grandma's closet."

"Is she a hooker?"

"No, a concert pianist. You know that!"

Rob turns the key and the motor purrs. "Where to?"

I take his hand. "Anywhere but here."

"Let's go look at the gym."

"Do we have to?"

"This is your prom, Morgan, and you've paid for it, and for me. But I have something planned for later."

"You do?" I'm intrigued. I tiptoe my fingers up his arm, over his shoulder, and onto his neck. I'm hoping he's ticklish there.

He squirms away. "We have an obligation, okay?"

"Dammit!" I hate it when he's right.

A few other couples are milling around outside the school, but it's hot so we go in. Rob doesn't want to pit out his tux. It's sort of a miracle he found a tux in the space of a week.

The theme for the evening is "Love in Outer Space," and I have never been so embarrassed for my class as I am at that moment. The gym is silly. There are large hearts covered with tinfoil hanging from the ceiling (a *long* way up there), with antennae on the hearts, and a big space-ship in the corner with red hearts pasted on it. Someone's made a big moonscape on another wall, complete with aliens holding hearts over their heads. Couples are laughing behind their hands.

Rob glances around, then turns to me. "So what do you think sex is like without gravity?"

I snort. Then Rob laughs at my snort, and pretty soon we're holding each other up because we can't stop. It feels so good to hold him, even if we're trying not to fall down. Finally, when we're both back to giggles, Rob touches my cheek. "Hey, I didn't kiss you yet."

"No, you didn't." I've been so busy worrying about my family, and then about Jessica and Derek, that it hasn't even crossed my mind. "Get to it."

Rob pulls me behind the love spaceship. "Are you sure? It seals the deal about us being a couple, you know."

"What's your point?" I hope my all-teeth-showing smile is enough to convince him. "We're behind the love rocket. What other conclusion could you draw?"

"It's not a love rocket, dork! It's a love hovercraft. I'm the one with the love rocket."

I stick my tongue out at him. "Whatever."

"You should watch what you're doing with that tongue."

And then he kisses me, good and long and hard. So very, very good and long and hard. I kiss him back with equal force.

We finally come out from behind the spaceship, and the gym's deserted.

"I bet the banquet's started!" I pick up my skirt so I can go a little faster, and Rob hustles behind me.

We get to the caf just as they begin serving. I hope it's something other than regular school food. The decorations are red and silver, with spaceships hanging from the ceiling and hearts dangling from the spaceships. Across one wall is a banner that says, "Love flies to infinity." Who makes this stuff up? Our name cards are at a table with two seniors, Annette and Roger, and they're already there.

"Hey, Morgan!" Annette's dress is one of those ruffly Scarlett O'Hara numbers. She looks like a chrysanthemum.

"Hi, Annette. Hi, Roger."

Roger looks confused. "Hello. Where's Derek?"

"This is Rob Jensen, Roger, Annette. He's my date tonight."

Rob smiles his charming smile and sits down after he pulls the chair out for me. I whisper, "Manners make me hot" and I see him grin. The dinner is average, but still better than regular school food. The conversation is fine, if a shade on the nerdy side. Once we're done eating, Rob holds on to my knee and I keep my arm tucked in his.

A band starts in the gym right after the dishes are cleared. I've been absorbed, for some odd reason, by Rob and Roger's conversation about rainfall totals in the Panhandle, so I haven't noticed that people are floating toward the sound. But Annette has.

"Roger, shall we dance?" She has a kind face, and she's really sweet to him. Maybe I should hang out with her.

Roger looks at her with all the love in the world. "Certainly, my darling." He takes her elbow as they stand, then propels her off toward the dance floor.

Rob watches them go. "Are you friends with them? They seem okay."

"It was luck of the draw, but they're nice, aren't they?"

"You could do worse." He darts his eyes in the direction of Jessica and Derek, who are sitting with some of the popular seniors. Or seniors who think they're popular. If I was Derek's date I'd be bored. Rainfall variations, while not entirely exhilarating, are better than all-star wrestling.

Rob's hand is in mine. "Shall we go?"

"With you, I'll go anywhere." I hope he'll take the hint, but he heads toward the gym. Dammit.

The gym's filling up, tuxes and dresses of all shades, and the band has a smoke machine pouring out foggy haze. I hate those things. They're cheesy and they make me cough, plus they smell like B.O. The band's name is 4Play—my guess is the parents' committee didn't understand the pun—and they seem to be into '80s hair-band music, so it isn't good for dancing. People are pretending, though. Rob and I watch and hold hands.

Then the band tries something slow, and I realize it's "Wonderful Tonight" by Eric Clapton. That song is almost older than my dad.

Rob holds out his hand to me. "Will you do me the honor? I love this song."

Cheesy or not, I've been waiting for this moment all night. "My pleasure."

We wander out to the dance floor and make ourselves a little circle. Our feet go around very slowly and we follow them, folded together. It's the closest to perfect I've ever felt. Even on my birthday, I didn't feel this perfect. I don't notice where Jessica and Derek are. I sure as hell don't care.

Then someone taps me on the shoulder. "May I cut in?"

It's Tessa. In a tux, just like she said she'd wear. She looks good. And she looks like she's got something on her mind. Last week we laughed about it in study hall, but I didn't think she was serious. This is Central Nowhere.

Rob's annoyed we'd stopped dancing. "Who are you?"

I'd forgotten to fill Rob in on the possibility that a woman in a tux would ask me to dance. Whoops.

"This is Tessa Roberts. Tessa, Rob Jensen."

Tessa sticks out her hand. "I'm honored to meet the person who stole Morgan's heart." Rob shakes her hand, just a little, and she gives him a slight bow. "Could I borrow her for just a second?"

"Uh ... if she wants to be borrowed."

It's the ultimate question.

"Sure." I give Rob a quick kiss. "I'll be back." He scowls. "You dork, I'll be back!" I pinch his ass. Then he smiles. Sort of.

Tessa drags me off by my hand. When I look over my shoulder, I see Rob walking back to the sidelines. No one's watching him, but everyone in the place is looking at us. Staring, like they've never seen either of us before. And why wouldn't they be? We're making history. I can hear the shards of my social handicap hitting the gym floor. I'll be back to nine zillion after this.

Tessa pulls me to the center of the dance floor.

"What are you doing? I wasn't serious when I said I'd dance with you!"

"Oh, whatever. Let's dance right here in the middle." The fact that there are no people around us for about twenty feet doesn't seem to bother her. People cleared away as soon as we showed up. The band twangs through Clapton, not watching the free show on the dance floor.

"Tessa!"

"It's okay." She sticks out her left hand, like Fred Astaire in a classic dance position, and places the other one on my waist. I put my right hand in her raised one, and the left one on her shoulder, and we dance. She even leads. I thought only parents could dance like this.

"Where did you learn how to do this?" I smile at her and she smiles back, like dancing together is the most natural thing in the world.

"My dad's a great dancer."

The song is almost over, but Tessa waltzes me around the cleared-out floor, humming. She puts her cheek next to mine for a second and whispers in my ear.

"Do you regret it?"

"Regret what?"

"You know."

I don't answer. She pulls her mouth away from my ear and gives me a look that says, "Please don't say yes."

I have no idea what's going to come out of my mouth.

"No."

"Really?" Relief washes over her face.

"No." I smile.

Tessa looks happier than I've ever seen her, and it's contagious. I stop paying attention to the faces of the people in the crowd and start to laugh. Tessa's eyes get wide. But she can tell it's a good laugh, not an embarrassed one, so she starts to laugh, too. Eventually we're guffawing our way around the room. I'm laughing so hard I'm crying.

The song ends, and Tessa leans in and places a gentle kiss on my lips. "Thanks for the dance. You did a good job following my lead."

No one in the whole gym moves or talks.

I'm not surprised. I'm not grossed out. I'm just not interested.

Tessa turns away and barges out the gym doors that are supposed to be blocked while Mr. Solomon hollers at her not to do that. I go to find Rob, which isn't hard, because he's right there when I turn around.

"Are you nuts?" Rob's voice echoes, because the gym is silent as a church.

"I didn't do it, she did." I keep walking toward the ring of people around the dance floor, and the murmurs of shock ripple around us. Now everyone's talking, but not to me and Rob.

"She kissed you! And you're *my* girlfriend!"

"*She* kissed *me*. I didn't kiss her back."

I didn't even want to.

"So are you her date now or mine?" His whole body is tense.

I smack him on the arm to remind him it's me, his buddy from facing-baby-food. "You are a true dork. Whose date do you *think* I am?" He relaxes, but only a tiny bit, and I answer for him even though he frowns. "Just yours. Would you get over it? She and I are cool. Could we get something to drink? All this excitement makes a girl thirsty." He glares, but takes my hand. I smack him again.

No one's spiked the punch yet, judging from the taste. We get cups and head back to the sidelines. Every time I walk by a group of people, I hear the hiss that means people are talking. Rob and I listen to a few more '80s cover tunes, and we dance a bit. He's not the greatest fast dancer, but it's fine. No one is a particularly good dancer—it's high school.

Rob's regained some of his good cheer because I've done my best to hang on his arm and give him my undivided attention, like a good girlfriend. The next time a slow song comes on, he grabs my hand. "Can I show you the surprise I brought you?"

"Sure. Where is it?"

He's trying to look mysterious. "That's the thing. It's not here."

"We can leave now? Groovy!"

The sponsors stop us at the door, and Mr. Gettleson looks sternly upon us. He is a hard-ass in the best tradition of hard-asses. "You realize, if you leave, that you can't come back."

"Yes, sir. We realize that." I do my best to look solemn.

"All right then. See you at the post-prom party."

I smile politely. "Yes, sir."

I hope not, sir.

Rob and I find the GTO and take off. The night is coolish.

He starts the car, then turns to me. "You're sure you want to be with me?"

"Of course I want to be with you! It was nothing!"

"A kiss between girls isn't nothing in this neck of the woods."

I pretend to dope-slap him. "That may be true, but that kiss meant zero. Zip. Nada. Nothing. Trust me, will you?"

"All right then." He pulls out of the parking lot. "Do you want my jacket?" He pulls the car over and slips the jacket off. Now I have proper prom attire: prom dress and tux coat, with hooker shoes to boot. Rob pulls back onto the road and drives out of town. We're heading west.

I snuggle into his coat. "Where are we going?"

"Sit back and relax. It's only eleven, so we still have six hours of no worries."

So I sit back and relax. Rob turns south, and I see the shadow of the hills in front of us. The car climbs up the hill, then Rob parks where I park for my shouting sessions. He leans over and kisses me. "Close your eyes." I obey.

He gets out, and I hear the trunk open and close, then some rummaging, banging, and cursing. I have to sit with my eyes closed for a long time, but I don't mind. I'm cozy in his coat, and sleepy.

I hear one last thump. "Okay, open your eyes!"

Rob has a table, two chairs, a bottle, two tall glasses, a small camping lantern, and a CD player. The table even has a tablecloth on it. I open the door and step out. "What's all this?"

"This is our prom. Happy end of your junior year."

"What a cool surprise."

He bows low, then holds out his hand to me. "Would you care to join me?"

I accept it and he leads me to the table. "Of course."

Rob puts on something quiet and soft, then pops the cork on the bottle. It shoots into the darkness. After he pours the champagne into the glasses, he hands one to me.

"To us, Morgan. To fun and dancing. To this valley. To kisses and laughter. To letting my dick go soft someday."

I almost spill my glass because I bust out laughing. "To us." I curtsey. "Thank you for tonight."

"You're more than welcome."

We toast and drink. Then we kiss, long and deep and slow. And dance. And kiss. And dance.

At some point, during some slow song, I notice Rob has his hands all over me, which is all right, because I have my hands all over him.

We occasionally use our lips for something more than kissing.

"Rob, why did you come back?"

"What?" His face is buried in my neck.

"You got to go away. Far away. I would kill or die for that opportunity, so I don't know why it's worth sticking around Central Nowhere."

Rob brings his face out of my neck. "Well…two reasons."

"And they are?"

He lets go of me and sweeps his arms wide to the dark valley. "I love it here. I love seeing one other car on the road for miles and miles. Or seeing three people—instead of three hundred—in one afternoon. I love the cows, the space, and this sky." He points up at the stars. "Look at that. They're like a carpet of shiny silver thumbtacks on a black bulletin board."

"Dude, you really need help with your similes."

"Either way, I don't know why anyone would leave."

"Was it like this in Argentina? Big and empty?"

"Kind of. They have more people and ranches, and it's greener there. And they speak Spanish."

"Duh!"

"But it's not here." He pauses. "This is my place." He looks dreamy and soft.

"Those are better reasons for sticking around than a house and a truck."

He's puzzled. "Who said anything about a house and a truck?"

"Those are Derek's reasons for staying." I take his hand. "What's the second thing?"

He kicks the dirt we're standing in. Grandma's shoes are already toast from dancing out here on the hill, and his kick doesn't make them any better. "You won't tell?"

"Who would I tell?"

Big pause. "I'm scared."

"Of what?"

"What if people in other places are mean? Or the cost of living is too high? People might forget me if I leave. And what if there's no sky?"

"If you're scared, how did you manage to stay in Argentina for a year?"

He won't look at me. "Lots of tears."

"No way."

"The first month I was there, I cried myself to sleep every night. After that, I got used to it, but … it was hard."

I think he's expecting me to yell at him for being so un-macho, but I pull him back to me and hug him even closer than we were before. "Even though I think you're nuts for coming back, I'm glad you're here."

"Me too." Rob traces my back with his fingertips. It's exquisite. "You want to hear my ultimate dream?"

"Of course."

"I want land in Cherry County. Out in the Really Big Empty."

"That's a wasteland!" Cherry County has more cows than people in it.

"That's why there are satellite dishes. Think how big the sky would be there." He touches my cheek. "You could always come with me."

I let go and step back, so I can see if he's serious. "Cherry County is a long way from New York. I don't think I can write fortunes—or the Great American Novel—way out there."

"You'll come back someday. Everyone does."

I stomp my foot. "What the hell do you know? I won't!" The heel of Grandma's shoe snaps.

He's chuckling at my crabbiness. "Relax."

"You're making fun of me."

"No, I'm not!"

Nobody takes me seriously. The one person who did contributed to my mother's death.

I yank off his tux jacket, throw it on the ground, and stomp on it with my hooker shoes. "I will *not* give in, I will *not* give up, I will *not* sell out, and *I will not come back*!" I jab my finger at him, even though he's backed far away from my fit. "I'm bigger than Cherry County, I'm bigger than this sky, I'm bigger than the universe, and I will not give up my dream!"

Nobody can be bigger than the universe.
But it doesn't mean you don't want to be.

He picks up his tux jacket, once I realize what I'm doing and step off it, and brushes at the dust with some force. "Whatever, Drama Queen. You'll meet cool people and do fun things. It'll be great. But then you'll come home." He brushes some more, harder and harder.

"You don't know that!"

"Yes I do. And if I lose my deposit on my tux I'm gonna be pissed."

"No, goddammit, you do not know it! It's…a soul thing. My soul is too big for this fucking little place!" I stomp my hooker shoes again, and the other heel breaks. I won't be Grandma's favorite grandchild after this—like I ever was, since it was all a hoax anyway. I push her out of my mind. It's not the time.

"So what about us regular folk with regular souls?" He keeps brushing.

"Excuse me?"

His voice is icy calm. "Your dream happens to be two thousand miles away. Big deal. You're no different than the rest of us, trying to figure out what to do." Rob puts his jacket back on. "Your dream's no bigger than mine. Some people's dreams are just closer to home."

I stomp off into the darkness on my broken shoes, and Rob doesn't follow me. The crickets are louder than I've ever heard them. When I sit down on the ground, I hear something rip somewhere on my dress. It figures.

I don't know whether to laugh or cry or shout. Or just give up.

It's quiet for a long time. Then I hear Rob call. "Morgan?"

I don't answer.

I can hear him chuckle. "Can you come back to Central Nowhere for the moment? I won't say anything else. I promise."

Suddenly I'm more than a little embarrassed. If I could walk home on my broken shoes, I would. But I stand up, dust off my ass, and make my way back to the lantern light.

He's smiling a gentle smile. "The bad thing about dreaming, or arguing, is it makes you forget where you are." He holds out his hand. "Can you come back to the hill for now?"

I'm not sure, but I'm shivering. "Maybe. If you let me inside your coat." It's cold.

He opens his lapels and I walk in. When he cuddles me close, I let myself relax. Just a little.

"Are you done having a fit?"

"Maybe." I say it to his chest, because I'm still too embarrassed to look at him for long.

"You'll know where me and my dream are, if you want to find us."

I mumble to his chest. "If I ever come back, I'll think about it."

He tilts my chin up so I'm looking at him. "Can we go back to what we were doing?"

But I look away. "If you still want to kiss me."

It turns out he does.

We make out until four—we'd set Rob's phone to go off—so we can pick everything up and make it back to my house by five. It takes a while to drive back from the hill. The sky's beginning to get light and the robins are chirping up a storm by the time we get to town.

Rob gives me a serious look as we pull up outside my house. "I need to ask you something before the night's over."

"Sure." I'm warm and dozy.

"What are you going to do about Tessa?"

I give him a sleepy look. "Didn't we go over this?"

"She kissed you, and you're supposed to be *my* girl-friend."

Now I'm wide awake. "Did you not listen? She did it without my permission!"

"You didn't exactly shoo her away, did you?"

A good point, I must admit. And he doesn't even know about the first kiss. "It was a dance and a kiss. So what?"

He stares at the steering wheel. "I've kissed your lips all night long, but a woman kissed them, too. That's just wrong." He shakes his head. "Flat-out wrong."

"Excuse me?"

"It's ... sick. Against nature."

I have to let those words sink in.

Then I explode. "Stuff it up your ass, you small-minded bigot!" I'm not prepared for my anger, but it's so white-hot you'd think it was PMS time. "If you can't deal with me and Tessa being friends, we don't have anything to talk about."

"Fine." Rob opens his door, storms around the car, and yanks mine open.

I leap out of the car. "Such nice manners, Mr. Morality. Call me when you get a clue about the world outside of Central Nowhere." I slam the door so hard the car shakes as Rob strides back around it. The GTO backs out and squeals away.

"She's a better kisser than you are!" I scream it at his taillights. It's not true, but right now I don't care.

Fuck people. Fuck my family. Fuck love. Fuck it all.

Do not let great ambitions overshadow
small success.

Shanghai Garden, Madison

My great ambition is to survive school today. On Saturday
night, it didn't seem like such a big deal. I was with Rob,
after all—no question about who did what to whom. I
was safe. But this morning, I can't eat breakfast. It's one
thing to watch girls kiss girls on TV. It's another thing to
watch them kiss in your gym.

I write *It's not a big deal, but it is* or *I am the dumbest
girl on the planet* on every dirty car I pass on the way to
school.

When I'm at my locker, Mason Anderson whips an
empty water bottle at me and shouts "Dyke!" Everywhere
I go, I see the look that says, "How gross are you?"

I don't know how Tessa does it.

At lunch, the sideways glances are intense. While we
eat, Ingrid looks at everyone looking at me. I'm not sure
why she's brave enough to be my Girl To Sit By, but I'm
really glad she is. I try to focus on my food, but it doesn't
work.

She swallows. "Holy shit, how could you let Tessa kiss you?"

"I didn't have a choice. She just did it."

"Ballsy."

"It's not like we played tonsil hockey." This time.

"It was weird enough that you brought someone other than Derek. And then it got weirder watching Jessica and Derek dance together. And *then* you danced with Tessa, and then she *kissed* you. It was all anyone could talk about at post-prom. Speaking of that, where were you?" She gives me a sly grin.

"We went dancing in the country."

"Oooh, sex between the corn rows!"

"Shut up!" I don't say that the night ended in a complete mess.

"You haven't done him yet?" Another wicked grin.

"Oh, please." I try a bite of cheeseburger, but I can't get it down.

"You seem extra hot for him."

"Possibly. But the horizontal bop makes things … complicated. I don't want to make the same mistake twice."

"Sex with Derek was a mistake?"

"I wanted to lose my virginity, that's all. Sex with Derek was awful. He has a little peepee."

Ingrid giggles. "Let's be sure Jessica hears, in case she's tempted to sleep with him."

"Hears what, Ingrid?" Speak of the devil.

I turn around to give her a glare. "Nothing. We were just discussing prom."

Jessica gives me one in return. "Girls kissing girls? Nasty."

"I'm sure you thought so." I stand up to put my lunch tray away.

Jessica sniffs. "Me and about a thousand other people!"

"Guess it's a good thing I don't care about those thousand people. See you later, Ingrid." I give Ingrid a wave and Jessica the finger, which makes Ingrid laugh so hard she almost falls off the bench. Jessica is so shocked she can't do anything but stare.

I do care. But I can't. You know?

When I go to my locker, there's a Post-It note stuck on the door. All it says is "let's hear it for girls kissing girls!" The handwriting isn't familiar.

Then Martin hustles up. He's bothered.

"I heard about you in science class."

"I'm sure you did."

"Doesn't it freak you out that the entire school is gossiping about you? We're freshmen, we weren't even there, and it's the talk of our classes, too." He chomps on a cookie.

I slam my locker shut. "It is what it is. Where'd you get that cookie?"

"Cafeteria. Are you in love with her?"

"No. My love life is complicated enough with Rob."

He breaks his cookie in half and hands it to me. "I heard about that too. Someone told me you smacked Jessica at the pre-prom party because she brought Derek and you'd told him to stay home because you were bringing Rob."

"I did not smack her!"

"That's too bad." I can see he was hoping for a rebel sister.

"Why don't you go to class?"

Martin scowls. "It's not like I asked to be your brother."

"But you love me anyway."

"See if I ever share my cookie with you again." He walks off.

After school I'm home for about three seconds when the phone rings. When I look out the window, Tessa's waving at me from her kitchen.

"Are you pissed? I heard you were pissed." I can't imagine today was very easy on her, either. And I didn't see her because I didn't go to study hall. It was too nice outside.

"It was an impulse thing. No stress."

"Exactly. You looked way too cute, and it was just a teeny kiss." The windows are open in our houses, and her laugh comes through the phone as it drifts over our yards.

"You freaked Rob out. We haven't talked since prom."

"That's only two days ago."

I get stern. "And you can't kiss me, ever again."

"Why not?" There's still laughter in her voice.

"He thinks you force yourself on me. Which you do."

"But he needs to know he's got competition!"

"Tessa."

I can hear the disappointment. "I know. Just jokin'."

"See you tomorrow. And hey—did you put a Post-It note on my locker?"

"No. Why?"

"Someone did. And it said something nice."

"Must be another lesbian with a crush on you." She laughs.

"Must be."

"Bye, Morgan."

And that's that.

Be yourself and you will always be in fashion.

Hong Kong Seafood, Baton Rouge

I finally get up the guts to take Grandma her shoes. First I take Anne's car—who knew they'd let me have the car?—out to the hill. The dents from the table and chairs are still in the dirt, and I pick up shreds of paper tablecloth floating around in the grass. I don't even yell. There's nothing to say at this point, except *MY SECRET SEX FIEND LIFE IS OVER.*

A hawk floats by and circles six times over the fields. If I were a little more cracked, I'd swear he looked at me. He was probably thinking, "Gee, that girl is quiet today."

It's too sad to stay at the hill, so I'm at Grandma's house sooner than I plan to be. But I can't imagine it will be any less sad at her house.

When she sees it's me at the door, she can't open it fast enough.

"Honey bunch, come in! How was prom? It's been a whole week! Why haven't you been by with pictures? I want to see how the shoes worked!"

She's trying to act like nothing happened, and I can't

go there. When she reaches out to give me a big hug and a kiss, I move away so she can't touch me. The hurt on her face is obvious. Once I'm inside, she hands me a glass of iced tea and we go back to her screened-in porch.

I take a sip of my tea and decide to be polite. "I brought photos with me." I show her prints of the ones Anne took.

"You look absolutely lovely. And Rob's a very handsome guy. Did you bring back my shoes?"

"They're by the door, in a bag." I fetch them from the entryway, where I left them. "But … uh … something happened."

"Like what?"

I take out a beat-up shoe. "There was a slight fit of temper involved, plus a little dirt. Sorry about that."

Grandma examines the one I hand her, then reaches in and pulls out the other one. I wait for the disapproval, but she just puts the shoes back in the bag.

"They're just shoes." She pauses. "Can we talk about what happened in the closet?"

I cross my arms. "What else is there to say?"

"Obviously there's something, or you wouldn't be here today. Your powers of stonewalling are pretty strong." She has me there.

I glare at her, which I don't think I've done in my history of being alive. "So answer my question: what is there to say?"

"Nothing. But I could tell you I'm sorry a thousand times over. How about that?"

I take her in: her stylish hair, her regal bearing, her

sweet, lined face. She looks like she wants to leap out of her chair and hug me until I bleed, but she's not sure if I'll disintegrate when she touches me. This is the woman who loans me her car. Who lets me shout in her house. Who bakes me onion bread. Who buys me books.

A light bulb goes off. "You wrote a song for me, didn't you? 'Requiem for a Lost Girl.'"

Her smile is so pained it makes me hurt, too. "It was the only thing I could think to do. What can you say to a three-year-old who's just lost her mother? Your dad was keeping you away, and I was so angry with myself I had to pour the grief into something. Music was all I had."

Her eyes find mine. "What else can I do to help you understand how sorry I am?"

The question suspends itself the air, but then shifts, and becomes a choice.

Forgiveness or revenge.

Fullness or emptiness.

Joy or pain.

Without knowing what I'm doing, I'm on the floor in front of her chair, kneeling with my head in her lap, sobbing. She hugs me and strokes my head, and we both cry for a long time.

Finally all our tears are gone, so I stand up with a groan. "My knees are destroyed, and look what I did to your pants. They're covered in snot and crud."

She wipes her nose with her sleeve. "Big deal. You threw up on me once."

"I did?"

"It was Mother's Day, in fact, and it was a great reminder of how gross motherhood can be." She stretches in her chair. "I think you were five, so you couldn't help it. And your dad was letting me see you again, so I wasn't complaining." She smiles. "Don't tell anyone you saw me wipe my nose on my sleeve, okay?"

"Your secret is safe with me." I creak back over to my chair.

Grandma takes a ladylike sip of her tea. "So what else is new besides my broken shoes?"

"You're not mad about them?"

"Honey, I wore those shoes in 1988. I'm not going to wear them again. Back to what's new."

"School's almost out, and I'm still working at the Chow Barn. Nothing else." I drink a slug of tea. "What's new with your head?"

"They think there's something wrong with the arteries in it. Must be all the bacon I ate when I was younger." Her look is resigned. "The doctors say I'm lucky my brain still works. Strokes are hard on a person."

"Speaking of potentially broken things... I get those same kinds of feelings when I've got PMS."

She grabs my hand with force. "Make sure you get help! You don't want to do what I did." I've never seen her so insistent. "Do you understand me? Get help!" She winds down a little bit after another sip of tea. "The traveling wasn't good, either. I loved my job, but I was so lonely. I didn't show it very well when I got home, did I?"

I don't say anything. She sips, I gulp. We're quiet for a while.

I speak first. "Do you think Dad will ever forgive you?"

She's slow to answer. "I hope so. Even back then, I tried to make it up to him on the days when I was in my right mind. Things weren't always horrible. But when they were, they were extra awful. And then, with you and your mom...I can only hope. He's got lots of reasons to stay mad."

"It floors me that hormones can make a person so crazy."

Grandma gives me a sad laugh. "Why do you think you've had so much trouble with your crush at the store, or why that girl's had so much trouble with you?"

"Oh...good point." She has me there. "Speaking of hormones, I need some advice."

"About what?"

"Rob. He's pissed because Tessa kissed me at prom. We haven't talked since he dropped me off the next morning."

"Did you want her to do that?"

"She said it was an impulse thing."

"Did she slip you some tongue?" Grandma is grinning.

"Do I really want to know what you know about slipping someone some tongue?"

"Sounds like he has nothing to worry about. If he gets over it, he's as smart as he looks. If he doesn't, you didn't need him anyway."

"Right." I sigh. "I was hoping he'd be smart."

"He's just threatened. Men don't do well when their romantic territory is invaded."

"They're thinking with their little heads, aren't they?"

"You got it, honey."

And we laugh and laugh. It feels so good.

Forgiveness. Clemency. Amnesty. Absolution. Mercy. Compassion.

Pardon.

Eventually I drive home. When I get there, Dad and Anne are into it again, screaming and yelling away, and Martin and Evan have retreated to their rooms. Supper is burned into the pan on the stove—how cliché is that? I turn on the oven and put in a pizza, ignoring the shouts from outside. At least they're not in here with us, but they're polluting my back yard.

Maybe I can forgive Grandma for him. Maybe I could make some liquid forgiveness, pour it over both of them, and it could be enough. It's different for me—she's been nicer to me than anyone in my life. It helps that I don't really remember my mom.

But someday I'll have to forgive Dad. It's the same situation, isn't it?

Before bed, I brave the stacks of magazines around his chair and give him a kiss on the cheek. He's so surprised he drops the magazine he's reading.

"What's that for?"

"For your help with my report the other day. And for bringing me home from the shoe closet."

"You're welcome." He gives me a smile, a kind one,

with some love in it. I've never noticed before that he smiles just like Grandma. Then he takes another swig of beer, and I am dismissed.

It's a long, heavy chain, from her to him to me. I think I want to put my end down.

It's hard to be religious when certain people are
never incinerated by bolts of lightning.

Chinese Delight, Berlin

I get to Food Freak Out early today, and write *Suck it, fool*
over and over on cash register tape while I wait to clock
in. I haven't talked to Rob for two weeks and we haven't
worked together, either. It's not the post-prom glow I'd
imagined. This shift could be tough.

He walks by as I'm curling up my register tape, so I
keep my eyes on the table. He doesn't come back, so he
must be messing with backstock. As I listen for the click
that tells me it's time for work, I hear a THUMP instead. I
run around the stack of boxes to see what the noise is, and
Rob's on the floor.

"Hey!" I kneel down and shake his shoulder. Nothing.
"Rob!" I slap his cheek a little, once, twice, three times.
His eyes flutter, so I slap him a little harder. I can't lie and
say it doesn't feel good. It does. But I'm still scared that
he's knocked out on the floor.

"Wh-what?"

I jiggle his shoulder to help him wake up. "What happened?"

"I think I slipped."

He's lying in a puddle of soapy water, which I hadn't noticed because I'm too focused on his face. He sits up, slow as Grandma, and shakes his head.

"Are you okay? Should I call somebody?" I don't let go of his shoulder.

"Nothing's broken. Just a lump on my head." He feels the back of his head, then turns so I can see the lump. "Do you see any blood?"

I help him up and hold on to his shoulder to steady him. "Let me look at the rest of you." I walk around him, checking for scrapes or blood. "Nothing." I'm not sure what to do next, so I drop my hand. "Are you sure you're all right?"

Rob frowns. "How in the hell did that water get there?" Then he spots the mop and rolling bucket close to the stack of boxes. He rubs his hand over the bump. "My head's pounding, but I'll be fine."

Then it's time for our Awkward Moment. Nobody moves or talks. We just lock eyes. I want so badly to give him a kiss and hug, to comfort him and let him comfort me, but I hold my ground.

He gives first. "Thanks for the help."

"I've got to punch in and get up front."

He gives me a slight smile. "See you later."

He turns to leave and his apron rustles. Very slightly. But it rustles. I've never heard anyone's apron do that.

I'm curious. "Why does your apron make noise?"

He keeps walking.

Now I'm really curious. "What's in there?"

He stands with his back to me for a second, then turns back around and reaches into the pocket. In his hand he has all sorts of notes, on all different kinds of paper: register tape, Post-It notes, rain-check blanks. Fortunes I've left all over the store. The look in his eyes is hard to read. Then he stuffs them back in.

"I listened, Morgan. To everything you said."

He turns away and goes to find whatever box of crap he was looking for before he fell.

When I punch in and head up front, my head is still trying to wrap itself around the fact that anyone read any of those fortunes. I try to remember how many of them were about him.

When it's his break time, he comes through my line with his Dew. The store is dead except for Crazy Gus, still sober and sailing through the aisles with his tofu, refried beans, and teriyaki beef jerky.

"How's your head?"

"Sore as hell." He pauses. "We should talk."

"What do we have to say?" I can't decide between hostility or reconciliation, so I try for a medium ground.

He spins his Dew cap on the conveyor belt. "Well, you might say you're sorry for saying I don't have a brain."

"How could what you said about Tessa come from someone with a brain? Pretty bigoted of you, if you ask me."

"It's a new thing, okay? I wanted you to myself, and I thought she was in the way." He pauses. "And I was always told it's wrong. People like her, doing what she does. So cut me some slack, would you?"

I grab the Dew cap because he's annoying the hell out of me, spinning it like that. "So if I cut you some slack, what does that mean?"

"Well...we could be friends again." It doesn't sound like he knows whether or not that's a good idea.

"Maybe." I want to say, "Of course, sure, and let's kiss right now," but I don't.

"Until we decide we could be something else." He tries a little grin. "Until you go off to New York and realize the best thing you ever had got left behind in Cherry County?"

I throw a roll of register tape at him. "Don't mock me!" But I give him a little smile.

"I'm not mocking!" He hands the roll back to me with a little smirk. "I'm joking, but not mocking. And don't throw stuff. You could put an eye out. But it's better than hitting."

I give him a look. "We can be friends. But open your mind."

He glares back. "Open your own mind."

"It's plenty open!"

"If that's true, give me some time to get used to Tessa." Rob takes another swig of his Dew. "I found the kid who left the mop bucket out and showed him the knot on my head. I had him shaking in his shoes."

"That wasn't nice."

"I didn't yell that loud."

I feel myself blush. "Just out of curiosity, how long have you been picking up my notes?"

"Since I started working here." And he walks away.

The rest of the shift is cordial, which is nice. We might be able to get back to makeout sessions on the hill, provided he plays his cards right.

I still wonder about the size of his penis. And where his other tattoos are. I cannot help it.

Simplicity of character is the natural result
of profound thought.

Hunan Garden, San Antonio

When I get home from work the next day, I see that Evan's
left a notebook on the table. It's got all sorts of stuff sticking
out of it.

You will be accosted by a neighbor wearing elf ears.

Pad of paper from the table.

Beware of deranged and/or bitchrod lesbians
hidden in your town.

Paper airplane.

He comes back to the table. "Hands off. That's mine."
"Do you know what a lesbian is?"
"No."

Watch out for neighbors bearing Wild Turkey.

Post-It note with rain spots, and Evan's corresponding
note:

Watch out for wild turkeys! They'll attack you!

For lasting peace, remain alone for the rest of your life.

Sign from my door.

"Why are you keeping these notes?"

He gives me a calm look. "Because you wrote them. And they're really weird."

All I can do is hug him.

The more one knows, the less one believes.

New Chopstix, Lincoln

The more one knows, the more knowledge falls out of one's ears.

The more one knows, the more often they're called
a walking dictionary.

The more one knows, the less often one works in grocery stores.

I take my pad of Post-Its around the store and put the fortunes on a box of Cinnamon Toast Crunch, a cabbage, and
a twelve-pack of Diet Coke. Surprise! Here's some advice
with your caffeine. I'll have to tell Rob to leave them
where they are.

It's actually a good evening for fortune writing at La
Grocerie Bag, because it's a gorgeous night and nobody's
here. June is the best month in Central Nowhere.

I watch Gas & Ass through the doors, and I see Derek
and Jessica talking to the crowd outside. They've got their
hands in each other's back pockets, and I can only guess
that means she's familiar with little Derek now. Too bad
for her. But she'll like the house and the truck in Cen-

tral Nowhere. They'll have kids running around the yard before our fifth class reunion.

Rob's voice yanks me out of my G&A reverie. "Dammit, put the Winstons with the Winstons and the Marlboros with the Marlboros! You seem to have a serious issue with cigarettes."

I turn around and smile. "Dammit to you! They're both red, so who cares?"

He glares. "Do you want a flood of people returning cigarettes because they got the wrong kind? What if the pack is open and you won't take them back, and they want to argue?"

"Good point, Mr. Grouchy Assistant Manager." I run around behind him and make bunny ears over his head for the amusement of Jack, a new kid who's sweeping by the checkstands. Jack laughs. Rob turns back to the cigarettes after he rolls his eyes at me. I check him out, just for a second. He's still rockin' that ass.

"Girlfriend, I saw that!"

I know that voice.

Tessa's wrestling a cart out of the rack, and a girl I don't know is standing next to her—taller than Tessa, thin and pretty, with a long thick braid over her shoulder and a western shirt, like a cowgirl.

I rush over to the carts. "What's new, girlfriend?" It turns out Tessa's two-year college is in North Platte, so she moved to her aunt's house for the summer to take classes. I haven't seen her since school got over, so I give her a hug, and then it's the tall girl's turn to scowl. She should go stand by Rob. I glance at him, and he looks as crabby as this girl does.

Tessa laughs. "Don't call me 'girlfriend'! She pulls the tall girl over to me. "Morgan, this is Sarah. She's in the chef program with me. We came home to visit my folks and make them a decent meal. Lord knows they just eat frozen pizza."

She's right—it's all her mom buys, and I know because she makes it a point to come through my checkstand, thanks to the neighbor thing.

Sarah hesitates. I stick out my hand, to show I'm friendly, and she shakes it with force. "Is this the first time you've been to Central Nowhere?"

"Tessa and I came last weekend to meet her folks."

"Sarah is from Alliance, poor girl. Everyone knows Western Nowhere is worse than Central Nowhere. It's the boots." Tessa gives Sarah a sweet smile.

Sarah sticks out her foot to show me. "Our boots make us cooler."

To think cowboy boots are cool at all seems brave to me.

Tessa whacks Sarah on the shoulder in her traditional affection gesture. "I bought a pair, didn't I? You told me I look cute in them!"

"You do. Come on, your folks are waiting. We gotta get cooking, no pun intended." Sarah puts her hand on Tessa's shoulder. "Nice to meet you, Morgan. I've heard a lot about you." She looks more relaxed.

Tessa pushes the cart away. "See you in a sec." They wander off, talking about whatever food they're planning.

Good for her.

I go back to Rob and the cigarettes.

"Was that your girlfriend?" He says it as nicely as he can.

"As a matter of fact, it was."

"Looks like she's got a new one."

"Looks that way." I'm not giving him the satisfaction of bugging me.

He pitches me a carton of Winstons. "Here. I need to get to the salad dressing backstock."

"If I do it wrong, it's all your fault."

He shrugs. "Whatever."

I stick out my tongue. "Whatever."

"You're a pain in the ass, Morgan." He walks off, dismissing me with his hand.

"Just for you." I shout it at his back.

The sun's going down, and the night is soft and warm outside the big front windows. Next year I'll be getting ready for college. A year's not so long to wait.

Then I hear a *huge* crash, and an explosion of laughter. It can only be Tessa and Sarah. Tessa looks happy. But I'm gonna kick her ass if I have to clean up a mess.

About the Author

According to geographers, the American West begins at the 100th longitudinal meridian. Thanks to the fact that this meridian is the main street of her Nebraska hometown, Kirstin Cronn-Mills grew up six blocks east of the West. Eventually she moved to southern Minnesota, where she writes, reads, teaches, plays on an adult dodgeball team, and lives with her husband and son. *The Sky Always Hears Me* is her first novel. Visit Kirstin online at www.kirstin cronn-mills.com.